More Than a Slave

THE LIFE OF KATHERINE FERGUSON

MARGARET D. PAGAN

Library of Congress Cataloging-in-Publication Data

Pagan, Margaret D., 1941-
  More than a slave: the life of Katherine Ferguson
/Margaret D. Pagan.
      p.cm.
  ISBN 0-8024-3481-9
  1. Ferguson, Katherine, 1772–1853—Fiction. 2. African American women—Fiction. 3. Religious educators—Fiction. 4. Sunday schools—Fiction. 5. Women slaves—Fiction. I. Title.
  PS3616.A337M67 2003
  813'.6—dc21

                2003005536

1 3 5 7 9 10 8 6 4 2
Printed in the United States of America

The Negro National Anthem

Lift every voice and sing
Till earth and heaven ring,
Ring with the harmonies of Liberty;
Let our rejoicing rise
High as the listening skies,
Let it resound loud as the rolling sea.
Sing a song full of the faith that the dark past has taught us,
Sing a song full of the hope that the present has brought us,
Facing the rising sun of our new day begun
Let us march on till victory is won.

So begins the Black National Anthem, by James Weldon Johnson in
1900. Lift Every Voice is the name of the joint imprint of The Institute
for Black Family Development and Moody Publishers, a division of the
Moody Bible Institute.

Our vision is to advance the cause of Christ through publishing African-
American Christians who educate, edify, and disciple Christians in the
church community through quality books written for African Americans.

The Institute for Black Family Development is a national Christian orga-
nization. It offers degreed and nondegreed training nationally and inter-
nationally to established and emerging leaders from churches and
Christian organizations. To learn more about The Institute for Black
Family Development, write us at:

The Institute for Black Family Development
15151 Faust
Detroit, Michigan 48223

This book is dedicated to the memory of my father,
James Roswell Dorsey, Sr. who inspired me to write,
to Barbara A. Cooper who encouraged me to continue,
and to the many family members and friends
who supported me along the way.

If the Son therefore shall make you free, ye shall be free indeed.

JOHN 8:36 KJV

Then shall the King say unto them on his right hand, Come, ye blessed of my Father, inherit the kingdom prepared for you from the foundation of the world: For I was an hungred, and ye gave me meat: I was thirsty, and ye gave me drink: I was a stranger, and ye took me in: Naked, and ye clothed me: I was sick, and ye visited me: I was in prison, and ye came unto me.

Then shall the righteous answer him, saying, Lord, when saw we thee an hungred, and fed thee? or thirsty, and gave thee drink? When saw we thee a stranger, and took thee in? or naked, and clothed thee? Or when saw we thee sick, or in prison, and came unto thee?

And the King shall answer and say unto them, Verily I say unto you, Inasmuch as ye have done it unto one of the least of these my brethren, ye have done it unto me.

MATTHEW 25:34–40 KJV

Contents

Prologue

September 1772

*C*rossing the clearing that encircled several gray-brown slave cabins, Hannah Williams stole away from her plantation home in Virginia. She plied a steady course through the dense thicket, slinging aside stubborn tentacles of vines, tearing through the tangled path, and trampling layers of dead leaves. Juniper trees sifted the autumn sunlight. At the final stretch of ground, she saw the schooner that Tom had described: two masts with sails, brown body with red trim, and the LeQ__D,, she'd memorized, M O R N I N G G L O R Y, painted on the stern.

Alone, it floated at the pier. Should she reach it, that schooner would sail her to freedom. Close to her time to deliver, the trusted young servant dropped her small bundle containing food and a change of clothing and sat to rest at the river's edge. She perked her ears waiting for one last signal from Tom, who was concealed in the nearby woods. After a cue from the captain aboard the schooner, Tom's whistle cut through the trees to tell her *now!* Hannah stood, lifted her skirts, and darted through the low grass toward the pier that stretched out before her. Taking a deep breath, she raced down the pier to the narrow board that angled up to the vessel. With the Norfolk River stirring against her legs, she walked a tightrope up the board and landed on the schooner's deck.

Lumbering down a ladder, which led to a darkened passageway, she found a place to hide among the hogsheads of tobacco and stooped to wedge herself in. Soon the boatmen would board, and the benevolent captain would hoist anchor and steer the schooner on a course to the Chesapeake Bay. Quietly she waited.

When the schooner finally eased away from the wharf, away from the setting sun, Hannah breathed again. She pulled off her kerchief and mopped her sweating face and neck, reining in an urge to jump up, grab her skirt, and dance with joy. For now, the silent dust particles in a shaft of sunlight danced for her.

Hannah's excitement ebbed as night fell and she realized that the *Morning Glory* did not sail with the swiftness of her desires. She would be two days in her brig before reaching the bay and another week before docking in New York Harbor. Sleep, however, eventually overcame the young slave, whose skin was the color of the cured tobacco cargo with which she sailed. Resting her cramped legs against the wall of the dark ship, her tension melted away.

As each dawn's sun nuzzled over the watery horizon, Hannah felt the loosening of slavery's grip. She thought of her family, her older sister Patsy, whose melodious voice soothed the family at evening time. Patsy, into whom Massa's son pounded his youthful lust, had delivered three mulatto babies before her twentieth year. Hannah's young brother, Zack, spent his days fashioning slingshots from fallen branches for the boys to play with and made dolls from dry cornhusks for the girls.

Hannah pictured Samson, the only father she knew, bent and broken with gray-flecked hair, hiking alone down a dirt road. Everyone he loved had been bartered, sold, or snatched away. She saw him only at Christmastime or when slaves could visit their families on neighboring plantations.

Then her thoughts rested on her mother, Sowei—a tall, proud woman with wide hips and high cheekbones that cradled the bright eyes of the Mende tribe—already pregnant with Patsy when captured by slave traders in the Bight of Biafra. Discovering she was with child and figuring they could increase their profit, the traders gave her enough food to sustain her through the deadly middle passage. After reaching America and birthing Patsy, Sowei bore two more children—Hannah and Zack—with her man, Samson.

Sowei prided herself in learning to survive as a slave and stand with a measure of dignity while many stooped to a self-loathing shuffle. But the pillar of her pride crumbled when Massa sent her man, Samson, away, so that young Massa could sow his wild oats with Patsy. Sowei could love her children and teach them to survive, but neither she nor their father could protect them. Massa held the reins on their young lives. Only when Patsy became pregnant with the first of young Massa's offspring did Sowei begin to dream of freedom, though not for herself. She felt that she had been through all she could bear; too much of her life had already passed, too much of her energy already spent. Hannah. Hannah would be free. She had the grit to survive.

To help her daughter understand the possibilities and stir up the girl's yearning for freedom, Sowei took Hannah to meetings with slaves who plotted escape. At these meetings, Hannah met Tom. She fell in love with his warm smile, which dazzled in the light of the camp-fires, and soon embraced his passion for freedom and manhood. He often found her looking across the circle of hopeful faces at him.

"Is you thinkin' 'bout freedom, Miss Dunmore?" he would ask Hannah.

"Of course I is, Mr. Williams," she'd say, lowering her large, brown eyes. "What else would I be thinkin' 'bout?" They found each other charming, attractive, and irresistible. In a clandestine ceremony, they jumped the broom and were married.

Within months, Hannah tearfully confessed to her mother that she was pregnant, which broke Sowei's heart. Sowei yearned for Hannah and for Hannah's children to be free. The thought of another set of her grandchildren anchored to the ship of bondage; of their feet buried deep in sinking sand; of their limbs paddling desperately to survive; of their reddened eyes looking up at the white underbelly of a huge vessel with no way around it and a faraway light in the sky casting faint glimmers on their upturned faces burdened her. Yet, the burden lifted when Sowei came to the idea of *faint glimmers from a light above.* The idea took hold: *a light from above. Glimmers of hope from a light above.* She knew that the answer shone in that light.

Sowei firmly decided that all of her will, all of her pride, all of her prayers would be driven toward one goal—freeing her children; first Hannah, in spite of her pregnancy, then Zack. She, Samson, and Patsy would have to remain.

A strong wind rushed the schooner toward the ocean, causing Hannah's spirit to be filled like the billowing sails. And though she carefully meted out her food so it would last, by the fifth day hunger pangs gnawed at her. But her hiding place offered only the smell of tobacco, an aroma that assailed her wide nostrils the same way the inside of a barn does on a hot summer day. It sheathed her thick, dark braids. Then it seemed to soak through her coarse clothing, to sneak down her arms and legs, and to invade the toughened layers of skin on her feet. Now, it shrouded her as she struggled to breathe.

Hannah comforted her heart with thoughts of her family as her mind sought a way out of her prison. But this was not home. She had stepped out of love's shining circle. She was alone on this smelly schooner, sick at the stomach, going to a strange place to have her baby—without her family, without a friend. Her beloved Tom would never make it out, she worried . . . not after Massa discovered her absence. She might breathe her last stifling air on this boat.

When pains began to sear through Hannah's abdomen, she knew they would soon force her from her hiding place. When she heard herself scream, she prayed for God to protect her. Footsteps pounded the planks above her as her child began to push its way into the world.

"Where's that doc?" bellowed a boatman's gruff voice, penetrating her refuge. "A woman's down here, likely a fugitive." The boatman was someone upon whom the captain counted to keep his lips shut whenever the captain brought out a slave. Having that skinny doc on board heightened the possibility of slave cargo because the captain never knew what kind of shape these runaways would be in. Soon a tall, thin man wearing a thoughtful expression arrived and told Hannah to lie down. With deft hands, he received the baby from her womb. She heard a strong wail as he slapped the freeborn child across its wrinkled buttocks. Her baby. Tom's baby. A perfect girl she would name Katherine.

He later shoved a welcome mug of broth in her hand and gave her other things she needed to make herself comfortable. Cramped, weak, and sore, Hannah stayed out of sight, poking her head aboveboard for a few minutes each day. By the time the schooner maneuvered through a late, noon sun into New York Harbor, baby Katherine was three days old.

Hannah emerged slowly aboveboard to sounds she'd never heard and sights more spectacular than she'd ever seen or imagined. The wharves teemed with goods of every description—bales of cotton and wool; barrels of rice, flour, and salt; hogsheads of tobacco and sugar; chests of tea; casks of rum and wine. Boxes, cases, and packages of all sizes and shapes lay piled upon landing places or upon the decks of ships. There were trunks, sacks, coils of hemp, and men racing back and forth.

Stepping up with her baby, she walked warily down the plank on swollen feet, not wanting to stumble or fall or do anything to delay the feel of solid earth beneath her. The good captain who'd ferried her escape stood at the foot of the plank, smiling, waiting to exchange words with her, to make it appear that she was free and to avert suspicion.

"Are ye strong enough to make it to the Negro quarter?" he asked. "It's two miles north."

"No, sir. I cain't," she replied, weak, drained, and without her husband's love to sustain her.

"Then go with the doc." He tipped his hat and returned his pipe to his lips. Hannah's frightened eyes were drawn to the many carts being pulled in every direction through the noise and bustle and to the Negro laborers on the wharves, who moved cargo from place to place. More carts, drays, and wheelbarrows jammed the streets where workers moved, leaving scarce room to pass. Not knowing where to go or what to do, she finally heard the doctor, who had come up behind her, tell her to get into a cart that would follow his carriage. A smooth wave of relief rolled over her, and though she had no idea of where the doctor might take her, she had little choice since she had not yet recovered her strength, was unable to get her bearings, and had an infant daughter to care for. She, with her growling stomach, was at his mercy. Using all of her strength, she climbed reluctantly into the back of the cart and went with the doctor, as the captain had ordered.

Rolling on wooden wheels and drawn by an old workhorse with a driver atop the front seat, the cart trailed the fine carriage as its steed clopped a short distance along a street and passed an open food market where Hannah's eyes feasted on squash, turnips, beets, cabbage, and potatoes.

Dr. Jay Marion rode in the carriage ahead. His gloved hands tightened around the black bag he was holding as he considered his options. General Howe would arrive in New York soon, and the good doctor wanted to be well out of reach when the general set foot ashore. After all, the doctor was on to something, having learned about new medical conditions while treating Negro women. He yearned to go back to England to publish his findings. Privately, he had hoped the young woman aboard the schooner would develop complications following her delivery. Then, he would have found a way to keep her, as he had told the captain he would, and further his experiments. But she appeared to be recovering, which meant she would be of no use to his research. Thankfully, she would bring a few pounds to help pay for his return voyage to London. He would take her to a friend who could help him dispose of the matter.

Hannah cuddled Katherine as they bumped along the street, leaving behind the *Morning Glory* with its sails now furled against the mast. "If only you'd waited another week," she whispered to the sleeping baby, "I'da made it to the Negro section and found a place to stay! Now, I don' know what'll happen to me," she cried. "I wish Momma was here." The carriage drew up to a dry goods store. Behind it, the cart rumbled to a stop. Dr. Marion climbed out, adjusted his clothing, approached the door, and knocked sharply on it several times before a man opened it and welcomed him inside.

Hannah stared from weary eyes as the door closed. Not knowing whether to attempt a feeble escape or to be still and pray, she decided to pray and to wait for Tom. He would come. He would rescue them. She did not hear the doctor when, after a very long time, he emerged from the dry goods store with another man.

"What can you do?" asked the dry goods man, looking down on her as she lay propped and hungry in the cart. Hannah wiped her face and replied with customary abasement.

"I cares for things made of lace—dresses, scarves, linen—all that, sir."

"Hmmm," he uttered, rubbing his chin. "Good." To Dr. Jay Marion he said, "I'll give you . . ."

They turned away so Hannah, who along with her baby was being sold, could not hear.

It took all of her strength to climb from the cramped cart as Mr. Bruce, her new master, led the way through his dry goods store to a narrow stairway that led to a garret above. When she opened the door at the top of the narrow stairs, heat poured from the room. A dormer window slanted the sun's fading rays on empty, dust-covered crates that lined the opposite wall. Facing her stood a ragged pillar of bricks that led from the fireplace downstairs to the chimney. Dust covered the floor.

"Come down later!" Mr. Bruce called. "There will be food on the table to eat." Swollen, scared, sore, alone, and in tears, Hannah dropped to the floor with her baby in a room that was just about the size of the slave cabin from which she had so recently escaped. Her hope of freedom winnowed away.

Hours later, after she came around and had something to eat, she reasoned that the Bruce house had to be home; what else could she do? This was a strange, new place and she had to think about her child, who now made escape too difficult. So Hannah lit a candle and consoled herself, thankful that, unlike the crowded slave cabin, only she and her baby lived in this room, and at least it had a window!

Missus Bruce, a round, kind-looking woman, ruled the household with a Spartan hand. She changed baby Katherine's name to Katy, saying that "Katherine" sounded too proper for a Negro. After Hannah regained her strength, she rose early every morning to gather wood, light the little brick oven, bake biscuits, and prepare and serve breakfast. Afterward, Missus Bruce would go to the shop to help her husband with customers. Hannah carried baby Katherine with her in a basket as she shopped, ran errands, did laundry, swept, and dusted. Often, she cared for Ann Amelia as well, the Bruces' first child whose birth, according to the missus, created the need for a slave. During the course of the day, Hannah would periodically kiss the rosy brown cheeks of her own dear daughter, and on Sundays, they would go to church.

Chapter 1

Given to God

1779

*P*reaching from high in his pulpit to the white people seated in the main sanctuary, Pastor Mason lifted his voice so that it carried to the Negroes seated high in the gallery of the Scottish Presbyterian Church on Cedar Street, reaching to Hannah Williams as well. So much so, that tears rolled down her cheeks, dropped to her hands, and trickled onto her faded homespun dress, making dark splotches. Hannah's hand gripped the hand of her seven-year-old Katy, sitting beside her.

Slave traders stalked New York City daily, seeking slaveholders whose earnings had dwindled under the British military government in the Colony. Massa Bruce had been seen by a Negro servant from a prominent household pocketing money from Newton Woolridge, the slave trader within whose eyes burned the very fires of hell. Rumor said it was for an adult woman, and all the Negroes—sitting tall and still in the gallery despite the shivering cold—knew that most likely it was Hannah who was going to be sold. Whatever it was, they knew it was a herald of disaster.

When church ended, the white worshipers pulled their heavy coats and shawls around themselves and left, leaving the Negroes to linger freely in the gallery of the small, white-frame structure.

"Don't you worry, Hannah. We hopin' it ain't how it 'pears to be," said one man, holding his hat in his hand.

"We don't know what's gonna happen, Hannah, but we all gonna be prayin' fer ya," said an older man, as others nodded.

"Don't make no sense!" interrupted a flat-faced woman wearing a green dress. "Worrying 'bout whether you gonna get sold to a flesh merchant. Lord, it ain't right!" They all agreed, shaking their heads, "Ain't no right in it!"

At home that evening in their icy garret above Robert Bruce's dry goods store, Hannah, with Katy on her knees beside her, prayed a desperate prayer. "Lord, please don' let Massa tear me and my baby apart! Who gonna love her like I do? How her daddy gonna find her if she ain't wit' me? If I get sold and my baby get lef' behind, I wants to leave her in Yo' hands. She Yours, Lord, just like she mine. I'm givin' her to You."

She said to Katy in a husky voice, "Either way, if Massa Bruce sell me or if he don't, you in God's hands now. Wetchee and Sim will help you." Hannah cried, pulling her daughter to her bosom.

"Don' cry, Momma," Katy consoled.

Hannah got up and stuffed rags around the dormer window to help ward off the cold, then huddled beside her daughter on the straw-filled ticking that served as their bed. For the little one, a warming glow of colors surrounded her mother, a glow that leaped and danced and chased off the drab brown dullness of slavery. She saw her mother's love as a cozy flame and felt it whenever she was near. Sometimes she closed her eyes, allowing the glow to surround them both. Downstairs, the Bruces and their three children lay on quilts around the wood-burning stove in their store, to draw warmth from the last glowing embers.

Frost coated the windows next morning when Hannah arose. Dressing quickly, she descended to the kitchen to stoke the hearth. After serving warm porridge to the Bruces, she returned to the attic room to get her child, so they could eat what remained. Later, she stood at the kitchen sink washing dishes, while Katy played with spoons at the table nearby.

"Hannah!" called Massa from the outer room. At the sound of his voice, Katy jumped down from the chair and ran to her mother. Something in the way he called her mother's name frightened her, and she grabbed Hannah tightly around the waist while burying her head in her mother's skirts.

"No!" she screamed, holding fast to her mother. Tears welled up in their eyes.

"It's all right, baby," she said to Katy, tugging her thick braids. "We don' know."

"Hannah!" called Massa Bruce, raising his voice to its full force.

"Yes, Massa?" answered Hannah, wiping her hands on her white apron.

"No, Momma, no!" cried Katy.

In a moment, Massa Bruce's lean, gaunt frame filled the doorway. His lips lined up under a well-shaped nose, dark eyes, and a bushy, furrowed brow. His angry stare pierced Hannah's heart.

"Now!" he demanded, moving toward them as though to forcibly peel Katy's arms from around her mother's waist. Hannah pushed Katy behind her.

"Yes, Massa."

"Go up to Pearl Street," he ordered. "Search through the rubble from the fire and see what you can find. Bring back anything of value."

Several nights earlier, a fire beginning on the west side at Whitehall Slip had cut a fiery path up north along Broad Street to Broadway, reaching all the way to the college grounds. Five hundred buildings in all, almost a third of the city, lay in charred ruins, leaving distraught residents and business owners to search among the rubble for anything they could find.

Even as Mr. Bruce dispatched Hannah, he knew that Woolridge's agents lurked there waiting to seize her and drag her to the slave market for auction. But that was more palatable to him than having them take her from his shop. He never wanted a slave anyway but bought one because the missus wanted help with Ann Amelia. He went along with Missus because he knew she needed help and because he owed Dr. Marion money. The doctor needed money to leave the Colonies fast, so he had bought her.

Mr. Bruce stepped aside to let his slave pass, then blocked the doorway. Katy screamed hysterically, punched the master's thigh with her tiny fists, and ran upstairs to the attic room. From there she watched anxiously through the window, weeping and twisting her shirt. A pall hung like a dark cloud over the normally busy street. Gone were the sparrows that skittered among the leafless branches. Gone were the people; no one walked up or down the street. Not a single cart squeaked by. The last thing Katy saw through the barren trees was the red bandanna tied around her mother's head. When it disappeared, she clutched her rag doll, went to her bed, and tightly curled up there.

Out in the streets, beleaguered New Yorkers without means to flee the British-occupied city suffered through the virtual standstill of trade and services. The recent fire added to their burden as they searched throughout the once-thriving city for fuel and food.

Two days had passed and Katy still lay in the same position on her bed. Mr. Bruce called Pastor Mason from the Scottish Presbyterian Church on Cedar Street to come pray for Katy's health. The clergyman agreed and soon after was following Mr. Bruce up the narrow stairway to the garret. Pastor Mason pulled up a homemade stool and squatted on it—his knees almost touching his chin.

"I oft have prayed for such in Scotland," he mused quietly before bowing his head in a long, silent prayer for Katy. When several minutes had passed, the girl stirred and the reverend stood, bumping his head on the slanted ceiling.

Pastor Mason had seen this child and her mother sitting among the Negroes in his church, listening attentively to his sermons. He had marked them as a pair who loved the Lord. Now the mother was gone. These colonists with their slave system were sometimes more than he could bear. Like the cotters in Scotland's Highlands, he felt they had a right to be free. Soon Katy opened her eyes.

"Pastor Mason!" she cried weakly and raised herself up on her elbows.

"Let's go, Pastor!" inserted Mr. Bruce, clasping the pastor's arm and ushering him to the stairway. "I really appreciate your coming. I'll tell the neighbor's help to come look in on her now." They left, and Katy soon heard Miss Wetchee's quick, sure footsteps, followed by the daintier, more highly arched footsteps of Miss Sim, climbing the stairs to the garret. Sim held a wet cloth in her hand for Katy's forehead. An apple and a small paring knife bulged in the pocket of Wetchee's red-checkered apron. Wetchee, a pure African, had been captured as a young girl. The only thing she ever liked about New York was the apples, and she stole one whenever she could.

"Dey stole me, so I reckon I can steal a' apple o' two," she always said.

Sim knelt down, lifted Katy's head in her fair hand, and wiped Katy's face. Wetchee knelt beside them, retrieving the knife from her apron pocket and scaling small bits of apple, which she put to Katy's lips. When

Katy sucked a little then took the apple in her hand, Wetchee breathed easily. Sim hummed softly as she stroked Katy's arm. A little cry broke from the girl's throat, followed by deep sobbing. "She all right now," nodded the women to each other. Sim embraced Katy as the child wept, and Wetchee, remembering her own two children who had been taken from her almost at birth, sighed.

Chapter 2

Growing Up

1779–1781

*A*fter the selling of her mother, Katy's life seemed to hang like a millstone around her neck. Each morning her body's weight seemed to press her to the bed. When she finally could get up, her hands would feel heavy and her feet like cords of wood she could scarcely lift. Her thin shoulders sagged under the burden of her heavy heart. Sorrow rolled over her, crushing her words before they ever came out.

With breakfast over, Katy would climb on the stool at the kitchen sink, roll up her sleeves, and plunge her hands into the dishpan of greasy water. She'd clean and rinse the wooden plates, lay them on their sides, then carry the stool outside so she could stand on it to hang clothes. Next, she'd take the water buckets to the water cart at

Pearl Street, fill them, and lug them home. At a penny a gallon, she dare not spill a drop. She'd sweep the house with the heavy corn-husk broom and, following lunch, deliver dry goods to Massa's customers who could not come into the store. When the day ended, if she had a free moment, she would call on Miss Wetchee or Miss Sim.

At night she'd fall into bed dead tired and remember things her mother had told her. *Your momma named Hannah Williams and your daddy named Tom Williams. We was slaves in Virginie and your grandmother, Sowei, had a desire that we be free. We planned to get away on a ce'tain schooner that dock at the wharf near the Dunmore plantation. We say if one of us could not get away, the other was to go on and we would meet up in New York. When we found out I was spectin' a chile, we didn' change our plans. I got on the schooner when it came, but not Tom. In all the tears and 'citement, you borned yourself on the schooner. All I could do was lay there and holla. A white doctor named Marion help me, but he sol' me back into slavery when we got to New York. But by God's grace, Tom will find us and we will 'scape again together. If somethin' happen to me, I'm leavin' you in God's hands.*

Thus Katy soothed herself with thoughts of her mother and welcomed the comfort she received from her mother's friends, Miss Wetchee, Miss Sim, and Mr. Hendricks, the Negro cart man. The load of sorrow had begun to lift when, without warning, the Pettibones—next door—moved away, taking with them the beautiful Miss Sim. Katy had always looked forward to Sunday mornings when, before church, Miss Sim would come over. She'd tuck Katy's woolly hair firmly under a cast-off bonnet she'd brought, then with a clump of lard she'd draw from her apron pocket, wrapped in waxed paper, she'd lovingly rub the dryness from Katy's face and hands. Afterward she'd lace Katy's handed-down shoes, which were always too small or too large, then stand back, look at Katy, and say, "There! Now you look like a proper young lady. Go on now. Go to church; sit next to 'Liza."

Imagining that she looked as beautiful as Miss Sim, Katy would smile as she'd skip to church, climb the ladder to the gallery, and slide in beside Miss Eliza.

"How you today, Katy?" Eliza would ask, patting her hand.

"Fine, thank you," she'd say.

Now slavery's wide net had dropped over Sim, adding to the lump of pain in Katy's heart. She began to spend her Sundays walking the streets, kicking stones she pretended were slaveholders. Her mother's friend Mr. Hendricks rarely came around, and she refused to go with Miss Wetchee to the John Street Methodist Church on the other side of town.

Chapter 3

The Fulani Girl

1782

*O*nce Miss Wetchee insisted that Katy go with her to the Methodist church for "homecoming." They met many people, ate lots of food, and felt the bonds of kinship and experience draw them together in loving accord. Sometimes the event would reach the heights of glory when a church member or guest was reunited with a lost, sold, or runaway kin.

This year, however, ended ominously. On their way home, they spotted a girl whose tangled hair shot out like an explosion around her sullen face. Her faded clothing hung as though from a skeleton. She ran like a rogue. Her deep and troubled eyes scanned the faces of each person she saw. Katy gripped Miss Wetchee's hand as the vagabond approached them, riveting her eyes upon their faces.

"Jus' act natu'al," Miss Wetchee whispered. Katy's heart pounded like a drum as fear surged through her. She wanted to run, but Miss Wetchee tightened her grip. Then abruptly the girl darted off.

"My Lord!" breathed Katy. "Who was that?"

"The Fulani girl," Miss Wetchee replied. Katy saw a tear roll through the soft, gray hairs that powdered Miss Wetchee's face. "She roams the streets in late evenin', searchin' for her sister."

"Her sister?" Katy asked.

Miss Wetchee sighed heavily, then proceeded to tell Katy the sad story. The Fulani girl and her older sister were taken from their home in Nigeria. While chained to a beam in the bowels of a slave ship, the two were able to keep in touch. When sleep came over them, the girls would tap with their fingernails on the beam. Night after night, they tapped out a rhythm that they made up and clapped with their hands at play like they did in their home, Nigeria. All along the middle passage, this tapping was the cord they clung to each other, and to life.

"When the dark cargo came to New York, the sisters got to see each other at the Meal Slave Market. But slavery's iron chains soon pulled them apart. The sisters were sold by themselves. This made the poor Fulani girl sad and she tried to kill herself a lot of times, by jumping in the river. Everybody could see she pined for her sister and for her homeland. Eventually, the man who bought the Fulani girl sold her to a tavern owner. She still works there in the back room washing dishes and sleeps in a closet."

After that explanation, Katy and Miss Wetchee walked in silence as black ghosts loomed before Katy's eyes. A crying child—lost, alone, disconnected. No momma to love her and to fix her plate, or comb her hair, or mend her dresses. There was no momma to kiss her, hold her hand, pray with her, or take her to church. Who would wiggle her tooth when it got loose and pull it, or say, "Here, let me help you wit' dat"? Or who would say, "Fix yo'self up!" when she cried? Or say, "Stan' tall like a Mende," when she slumped. "Dat white man don' own you. He jus' got you in his grip fo' a while." "I loves you, sugar!" No one to say any of these things. Disconnected. A wayfaring stranger.

Soon, gratitude replaced Katy's fear. When they reached home, she turned to Miss Wetchee and buried her head in her comforting skirts. "I miss Momma so much," she cried. "Miss Sim too." Miss Wetchee patted her.

"Don' worry, chile. God is wit' you."

"I'm glad you wit' me too. Thank you, Miss Wetchee." The following Sunday, Katy returned to the Scottish Presbyterian Church that she had attended with her mother. Yet, her anger toward the Bruce family remained.

Chapter 4

The Coin

1783

*K*aty turned eleven years old. On a cold, fall day, a yellow-brown woman with keen features, stepped from a carriage and came in to Mr. Bruce's dry goods store. "Do a girl named Katherine still live here?" she asked.

"Who are you, and what do you want?" asked Mr. Bruce, coming around the counter.

"My name is Sim. I'm looking for a girl named Katherine who lives here. Her mother was named Hannah. You may remember me, sir. Before the War, I served Mrs. Pettibone, next door. And now," she said, raising an eyebrow and twisting her parasol into the wooden floor, "I works for Cap'n Winchester at British Army headquarters."

He shot her a look of contempt that only grazed her; Sim knew she stood on solid ground.

"Wait here," he growled and disappeared through the draped doorway at the rear of the store. "Concubine," he muttered.

A pert, little white girl skipped out from behind a muslin-stacked table. From the waist of her soiled, white muslin dress hung a loose blue sash. "Hello," she chimed. "Katy's out back boiling water to make soap."

"Sarah!" called the little girl's mother, charging through the drapes in a frumpy housedress.

"Oh!" Mrs. Bruce exclaimed. "My husband said Katy had a visitor, but I did not expect . . ." Her voice trailed off as she looked Sim up and down, taking in every detail of her dazzling royal blue coat—with matching purse—covering a fine dress with a rose, gold, pink, and beige floral design. Sim's presence lit up the store like a bolt of silk.

Sim waited until Mrs. Bruce had gotten a good look before she spoke. "I hear that Katy is in the backyard. May I visit her there? I have only a little time."

"But *you* can't come through our kitchen!" Mrs. Bruce exclaimed.

"Ma'am, I *been* through your kitchen—many times. I was a friend to Hannah, yo' maid. Remember? Please, ma'am," she curtsied dutifully. "I haven't much time." Mrs. Bruce's full, round cheeks flushed bright red.

"Go on," she assented and gestured toward the doorway through which Mr. Bruce had gone. "Maybe you can talk some sense into the angry brat." Sim lifted her floral dress, revealing snowy petticoats, and then went through the kitchen. She entered a small, grassy yard with a sugar maple off to one side, and there she spotted Katy.

"Katherine," she called as she emerged from the back door. "Look how you have growed! You all growed up! Oh, baby! It's so good to see you."

Katy looked up from the steaming cauldron. Sweat poured from her smooth face and firm body, soaking the bodice of her coarse, brown dress. Her large brown eyes looked questioningly at the Negro woman who stood in the doorway. "Katherine"—the name sang like music in her ears. Her mother had called her "Katherine" when she rocked her to sleep on nights when thunder boomed and lightning seemed to strike the tin roof over their heads, when she got hurt, and when they were around Hannah's closest friends.

"Katherine, it's Sim."

"Miss Sim?" she asked as the name returned slowly to her memory.

"Yes, baby," Sim replied, stretching out her arms. Katy ran to her and took her hands.

"Miss Sim, I'm so glad to see you. You look so pretty." Katy held her soft hands as they smiled and looked at each other.

"You the picture of Hannah—bright eyes, smooth skin—though square built like I guess your daddy was." She lowered her voice, "You heard anything about your momma?"

"Nothing," replied Katy, looking down at the ground. Miss Sim raised her chin with her softly gloved forefinger.

"Is you all right?"

"It's hard wit'out my momma. Sometimes the hurt gets so hard in my chest that I can hardly stand it. I hate Massa." She paused. "Nobody call me 'Katherine' no more."

"I know, child. That missus changed your name to Katy. Said 'Katherine' sounded too highfalutin for a slave. But you and I know better, don't we?" Miss Sim laughed a drawing-room laugh and squeezed Katy's hands. Then her smile disappeared.

"Have they beat you?"

"No, they don't beat me. Massa is not as bad as some, and I do my work. But I still hate him."

"God! I wish I could stay longer. I'm working for a British cap'n now, and he at Brownjohn's saying good-bye to some people. The British soldiers are packin' up, gettin' ready to leave."

"Where they going, Miss Sim?"

"They going north, to Canada. Folks who fought on their side going too, even colored." She waited for her words to sink in.

"You going?" asked Katy.

"Yes," Sim replied, closely watching her. "Wetchee looking after you, ain't she?"

"Yes, ma'am."

"Hendricks too?"

"Sometimes."

"Look! I brought you a present." Sim lifted the flap on her royal blue purse. From it she withdrew two rosy apples.

"Here, Katherine," she almost shouted. Then she

added in a whisper, "Take what's in my palm. You got somewhere to put it?" Katy's eyes brightened when she saw that beneath the apples lay a shiny coin, an English guinea. "Go sit under the tree and eat one o' the apples. Then you can hide the money." Turning their backs toward the house, they sauntered toward the sugar maple, whose branches overhung the privy, and whose fallen, red leaves rustled under their feet. Sim opened her parasol with a great flourish as though to show it to Katy, while Katy bent down and pressed the coin into her shoe.

"As wet as your shoes is, it won't fall out."

"Thank you, Miss Sim! I never had no money befo'."

"Don't put that coin in church now!"

"I won't," Katy smiled. "I'ma save it."

"That's my girl." They sat quietly until Katy finished eating the apple, then started walking back toward the house, when Sim stopped and turned to look at her.

"You take care o' yo'self." Sim cradled Katy's face in her hands and kissed both cheeks. "Bye, darlin'. Remember Miss Sim love you." Katy closed her eyes so that she could hide those words in her memory.

Then she opened them: "Good-bye, Miss Sim. I love you too." And Sim was gone.

Her brightness floated away like a soap bubble gleaming in the sun, and poverty's gloom settled down in the backyards of clotheslines and barking dogs. In November, British armies, including four thousand freed Negroes, Sim among them, departed New York.

Chapter 5

Catechism

1784

*S*oldiers returning home to New York after the Revolutionary War found a desolate city where dogs and pigs roamed through garbage, where sooted buildings lined the poorly paved and darkened streets, where wharves rotted and sagged, and makeshift canvas houses dotted the landscape like giant anthills. Every street bore evidence of the fires and pillaging that ravaged the city while held in British hands. Many, including Ann Amelia, the Bruces' oldest child, had died of diseases resulting from poor living conditions.

But now the occupying force was gone. It was time to rebuild. New York's population had risen to its prewar level of 20,000 people, including the 3,000 foreigners who arrived each year but excluding the hundreds of

Africans still arriving on slave ships, bound in chains and imprisoned in pens at various holding places along the East River.

For Katy, the year 1784 was a time of preparation. The Bruces' two oldest children, eight-year-old Sarah and six-year-old Robert, attended catechism, and Katy took them. The teacher allowed her to sit in back of the class, where she listened. As the lessons progressed, a strange thing began to happen. The smoldering anger that seethed within her seemed to cool—not quickly but slowly, like the blaze from a pine-knot torch dying out.

Catechism seemed to lead her in a new direction. A quietness settled in her soul so that, even when Massa entered a room, she no longer grew tense and angry.

One day, as Katy was about to make batter bread with the children, she decided to lighten the chore.

"Little Massa, I wanna hear yo' catechism while I make this here batter bread." She removed the bowl of cold, leftover hominy from the icebox and placed it on the kitchen table. "Here yo' first question," she said, squaring her shoulders, lifting her head, transforming herself into Mrs. Graham, the catechism teacher. "Now, boys and girls, give me the answer to Number One: 'What is the chief end of man?'"

"Man's chief end is to glorify God and to enjoy Him forever," replied Robert with youthful enthusiasm.

"Very good," responded Katy, beating an egg with a fork while continuing to imitate Mrs. Graham's lesson. "Number Two: 'What rule hath God given to direct us on how we may glorify and enjoy Him?'" She found she liked imitating Mrs. Graham's speech as well. It made her feel closer to Mrs. Graham. "Take your time now," she added. Robert answered correctly.

"Very good, boys and girls. Do you know Number Three?" she asked as she sprinkled salt into an earthen bowl containing the cold hominy she'd mashed and the egg she'd whipped to a golden froth.

"Not yet. Can I go now?"

"Wait 'til your sister say . . . says," she corrected herself, "the 'postles' . . . Apostles' Creed. Is . . . are you ready, Sarah?" Sarah brought Katy a perfectly measured cup of white cornmeal from the burlap sack in the pantry.

"I'm ready." She recited the creed perfectly, then poured the cornmeal on the other ingredients while Katy stirred.

"Very good, Miss Sarah!"

"Thank you, Katy," replied Sarah, skipping to the hearth to retrieve the kettle of steaming water. "Katy, you sound like Mrs. Graham!"

I like talking this way, thought Katy.

"Little Massa, you must recite Number Two again. You know that every little jot must be just so. Missus Graham will tell your parents if it ain't . . . isn't exactly right." Under Katy's tutelage, the boy continued to recite the first two lessons in his catechism until he did so perfectly.

Katy drizzled hot water into the bowl and beat the mixture until a milky batter evolved, while Sarah heated a tablespoon of butter in the baking pan until it gave off buttery smoke and began turning brown.

"Hold the pan, Miss Sarah," Katy instructed, pouring the mixture into the well-used pan, while continuing to affect the catechism teacher's speech.

Assuaged by the promise that the bread would be ready when they awoke from their naps, Katy prodded the children to their bedroom, where they lay down without protest and fell asleep. Later when they ate the bread, Katy delighted in that she had imparted new life in the cold, leftover hominy.

Katy's success in repeating the catechism lessons gave her an idea that she needed to bring up with Massa Bruce.

"Bring it up on a Sunday after chu'ch," Wetchee suggested. "He'll be in a good mood den." Two weeks later on a Sunday afternoon, Mr. Bruce entered the kitchen clearing his throat. Startled, Katy jumped up from the chair where she sat looking out the window. There he stood in his black Sunday breeches, waistcoat, and shirt. Though she no longer hated him, the grim aspect of his presence never failed to intimidate her.

"Ah, Katy," he stuttered, thumbing his turned-back lapel, "thank you for helping the children with their catechism. I hope you will continue to serve God."

"It is my pleasure, Massa Bruce," replied Katy. "Sir?" she asked, deciding to test her idea.

"Yes?"

"Sir, if you will free me, I'll serve God for the rest o' my life." She looked at him hopefully, praying for a shadow of favor to fall upon her.

"Not a chance!" he replied with annoyance.

"Yes, Massa," she said, putting a lid on her dreams. *He think I belong to him, but I belong to God. Momma said so.* The young girl curtsied, and when she raised up, he had gone.

"Don' ever give up tryin' to git what you want," consoled Wetchee later.

As she lay praying in her bed that night, she thanked Mrs. Isabella Graham for letting her sit and listen as she taught the white children six weeks of catechism. She also thanked her mother for giving her to God and wondered what God wanted to do through her life.

Chapter 6

The Chase

1785

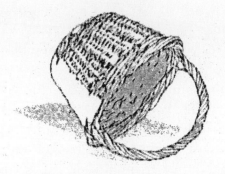

*A*s Katy continued to mimic the speech of Mrs. Graham, she found that it gave her more ways to express what she felt, thought, and wanted.

"Please, sir, may I have a half pound of dried currants?" she inquired one day at the Oswego Market. She remembered when she would have asked for "a bag o' li'l red berries" and the clerk would have asked, "What kind?"

"You make Winster Wake Cakes wit' 'em," she'd have said.

"Currants?" he would inquire.

"Das it."

"Fresh or dried?"

"Dried."

"How many?"

"Jus' a li'l bit." Annoyed, he'd put a few on the scale. "This many?" he'd ask.

"A li'l mo'."

"This many?"

"Jus' add three o' fo' mo'." Annoyed and impatient, he'd pour what he had in a piece of waxed paper.

"That's all you get."

"Thank you, sir." Then she'd have gone home and adjusted her recipe to the amount he had given her, incurring the wrath of Mr. Bruce. But today she said, "Please, sir, may I have a half pound of dried currants?" The clerk's eyes widened, then narrowed into slits.

"Know your place," he snarled.

"Yaasssuh," she drawled with a glint of humor in her eyes and waited patiently to receive the package. He gave her precisely a halfpound of currants. Outside, with her purchases tucked in the basket on her arm, she stuck out her hand from under the striped canvas awning surrounding the market. The shower had almost ended. Raindrops settled on the slick faces of chestnut leaves, and robins pecked around in a puddle. Soon her eyes followed a worm's captor to a high branch.

"Is de rain stopped yit?" asked a woman among the Negroes who came up behind her.

"Almost," Katy replied. "It's drizzling now."

Suddenly a man across the street called out, "Stagecoach coming! Stagecoach coming!" And the throng of shoppers stepped back. Cart men, lined up across Broadway waiting to unload their produce, pulled their two-wheeled, horse-drawn vehicles farther off the street so the larger stage could pass. Here it came, pulled by four thundering, dark brown steeds with flying black manes. As the coach slowed to make its way past, a young boy wearing a blue cap waved from the window, and the smooth, brown arm of a Negro woman sitting next to him reached to pull it back into the coach. Katy glimpsed the woman's face, noting the red bandanna tied around her head.

That looked like my mother, she thought, recalling the smooth, loving face she had not seen in seven years. *Could that be my mother in the stagecoach?* Her heart began to race. She had to know.

"Pardon me, ma'am! Pardon me, sir!" she called to people as she stepped out from the crowded planks that made up the sidewalk and took out running up the rain-muddied street after the stagecoach. Up ahead, the stage crossed John Street and barreled toward Fulton. Katy ran behind, splashing muddy water on her legs and skirts.

"Look where you're going!" called a man balancing with his umbrella as he stepped stone by stone across the muddy street. Darting past a horse-drawn wagon, Katy zigzagged and the flour sack fell from her basket. Then the eggs rolled out.

"Oh, Lord. I'm losing my supplies!" she cried aloud. "God, help me catch that coach."

The stagecoach bolted ahead. It was now two blocks from the Post Road to Boston. If it reached there, she'd never catch it. She spotted an older Negro man plodding along barefoot ahead. "Mister! Mister! Stop that coach!" The man turned his head and looked at her, never slowing his gait.

Katy charged with all her might, her eyes filled with excitement, chest pounding, perspiration trickling down her sides and between her breasts. To avoid a deep rut in the road, the stagecoach driver slowed the horses, which allowed Katy to get almost within arms' reach. She let her basket go and it flew backward from her, sailing high into the air like a kite before dropping back to the ground several yards behind, scattering her currants, her butter, and their wax paper wrappings. She almost reached the back of the stage. "Momma!" she called. "Stop! Stop! Momma!"

People stopped to stare. A white ruffian who'd been loitering in front of the candy store heard the commotion and began to move toward it like a cat stalking its prey. Soon his buddy joined him and they started running behind her. The taller one, wearing a red hat and a blue short jacket, caught up with her just as she reached the Post Road. He ran ahead, dashed in front, and stuck out his buckled shoe. Katy, with her arms outstretched and her eyes fixed on the stage, never saw him. She tripped over his foot, toppled, and slid to the ground. Lifting her head in a daze, she saw the stagecoach driver poise the whip high into the air before it snapped above the heads of the horses, who then broke into a fast gallop onto the Post Road.

The ruffians' loud laughter caused shopkeepers and their customers to come to the sidewalk and gawk. They saw the young girl pull herself up, scratches crisscrossing her face and arms. Horse-scented mud stained her dress, and stray dogs sniffed at her market items strewn in the muddy street. The older Negro man she'd seen earlier came over and handed her the basket. From inside his shirt he pulled a frayed kerchief, which he offered to her to wipe her face. Katy took it.

"Did you see that woman on the stagecoach wearing a red bandanna?" she asked in tears.

"Naw, miss. I didn't."

"That woman look like my momma!" she cried.

"No wonder you was running so hard. Is you all right now?"

"Yes, sir. Thank you, sir."

"I got yo' basket, though I'm 'fraid all yo' goods is gone. Can you make it?"

"Yes. Thank you. I can." Stiffly she turned to get her bearings, then started limping down the street—drenched, sore, disappointed, and carrying an empty basket. Merchants, shrugging their shoulders, returned to their shops.

"You can go out now!" a harried mother was heard calling. A door crashed open and out ran a boy with a stringy hard ball in his hand. He joined the ruffians as they walked up Broadway.

A bedraggled Katy reached home and explained to the missus that some boys had tripped her, that she'd fallen and hurt herself, and that all of the goods she'd purchased had been lost in the street. She apologized and showed Mrs. Bruce her empty basket, which the missus eyed suspiciously. Finally she shook her finger in Katy's face and shouted, "Don't let this happen again!"

"Yes, ma'am."

By the time Katy reached her room, her head had cleared, and something said to her, like the silent whisper of a wave sliding ashore: *Why are you still chasing after her? She gave you to Me.*

Chapter 7

Salvation

1786

$\mathscr{S}$lavery demanded that Katy lose her mother, that she lose ties with kin, that her lot be with strange people who did not love her yet controlled her every move. Still, Katy sensed the presence of a higher power. It was a desire sown in the heart of her grandmother, Sowei. A hope nourished by her mother, Hannah, and fed by her daddy, Tom. A way that Momma passed on to her. The way to freedom. It was through a higher power. Momma had taken her as far as she could, then given her to God. She would take the next step; He would not fail her.

Streaks of light fanned out across the Saturday morning horizon. Katy got up, did her chores, and then instead of taking a bundle of dry goods to deliver, she directed her path to Pastor Mason's house on Nassau Street. She was a breathless young woman feeling the urgency to confess her hard feelings toward Massa for sending her mother away. But that moment fled down the passage of time as she thought of knocking on a white man's door, even a pastor, even his back door. From her much-worn, faded bonnet poked her woolly hair. Only slaves wore colorless, homespun dresses of Negro-cloth such as hers. Repaired many times before she ever received them, her cast-off shoes slopped around her feet. In her rough hands she held no silk purse, embroidered handkerchief, or fringed parasol. Everything about her announced her as a slave. *Don't knock,* a voice told her. *Go away.*

But Pastor Mason had proclaimed in church on Sunday that all should come, all should accept Christ's forgiveness for their sins. Even those, she protested, sitting, like her, in the Negro gallery. *I must have the courage to knock,* she told herself, trying to steady her trembling knees. Shafts of sunlight shone through a red maple and landed on the door. *If I don't hurry, I'll be late getting back home to fix supper,* she chided herself. *Knock, knock.* Soon the door opened, revealing Pastor Mason himself in his polished black leather boots. She felt his eyes penetrate the top of her bowed head, making her breath stick in her throat. Gallantly she tried to steady her knees and release her voice.

"Have you come to talk about your soul?"

"Yes, sir." She kept her head lowered.

"Come in. Tell me your name."

"My name is Katy Williams. I know I's a sinner and I wants Jesus to save my soul. Before my mother was taken away she put me in God's hands, and He has protected me all these years since she been gone. Now I wants to know Jesus for myself," she blurted out.

"Come, sit at the table." The young girl ventured inside and sat down. "How did she put you in God's hands, Katy?"

"We were sitting in church, Pastor Mason. You were preaching about Samuel's mother and how she entrusted her chile to God."

"Tell me more."

"Well, sir," said Katy, beginning to relax. "Momma knew in her heart that she was going to be sold. I'll never forget the day. Her eyes filled with tears when we set out for church that morning. She cried when she heard your sermon. When we got home that evening, Momma got down on her knees with me beside her where she prayed and put me in God's hands. The next day Massa Bruce sent her somewhere so the slave catchers could get her. But I feel certain that she left me in His hands, 'cause He has comforted me."

"I see," responded Pastor Mason. "But how did she know to put you in God's hands?"

"There was a church near the Dunmore plantation where she growed up. The pastor's wife got her husband to allow slaves to sit in back of the church as long as they kept quiet and listened. That's what Momma said. So she kept quiet and listened. My father too. And my grandmother. And my Aunt Patsy and Uncle Zack. Momma named me after the pastor's wife, Katherine."

"Very good," he nodded.

"I know the catechism and the Apostles' Creed. Want to hear me say 'em?"

"That won't be necessary, Katy. Tell me, where do you live?" asked the pastor.

"On Water Street."

"Oh yes. I remember now. . . . Is there any special sin you wish to confess?"

Tears filled her eyes. "I have hated Massa for sending my mother away. The hatred had gotten so big in my chest that it choked me and took away my breath. Then I started going to catechism and it eased up. It seemed that the more I sat there and listened, the more that hatred faded away. I want it all to be gone. I want to be free of it so I can get on wit' my life."

As they bowed their heads together, Pastor Mason prayed. "In Your Word, Father, You say that all have sinned and fall short of the glory of God. But You did not leave us to suffer and to die in a state of sin, Lord. You gave us a way out through Your Son, Jesus Christ. Through His death, burial, and resurrection, we become reconciled to You, because He took the punishment for our sins. This young woman wants to cross the bridge from death to life, from sin to freedom in Christ, from old ways of evil to new ways of grace. In Your Word, You promise to welcome her. Katy, do you really want Jesus to be Lord over your life?"

"Yes, sir, I do. I want to stand before Him with a pure heart."

"Do you promise to consult Him before you take any action or make any decision?"

"Yes, sir. I want His leading now more than ever."

"You can lift your head now, Katy. Welcome to God's family."

"Thank you, Pastor Mason. Thank you so much." Katy looked up. "I don't know what I would have done if you had not a'cepted me."

"You said you knew the catechism and the Apostles' Creed. How did you learn them?"

"I sat quietly in catechism class with each of Massa's children and I listened to the teaching."

"Mrs. Graham's class?"

"Yes, sir."

"That's a credit to you, Katy. Can you read also?"

In response she hung her head. "Massa Bruce will not let me learn though I have asked many times."

"I'm sorry, Katy. Under the circumstances, I won't give you a Bible, but continue to learn by listening and memorizing. You will do all right. But tell me, why do you want the Lord's leading now so much?"

Katy hesitated. She did not want to embarrass herself. "I have a dream . . . I want to . . . be . . . I want to . . . open . . . a school for poor children."

"That's a noble dream."

"Thank you, sir." Katy felt like a bird freed from the snare of fowlers. She raised her head high and surveyed the kitchen, awakening to the beauty of the house. A shiny brass candleholder with a fresh candle sat in the middle of the table. From the fireplace hung gleaming copper kettles. Blue-trimmed plates stood erect in the cupboard, reflecting the sunlight streaming into a small window beside the door. Tidiness, thrift, and modest comfort characterized the kitchen, and the smell of finnan haddie did not diminish it. *This is how my house will look,* she thought, *except it'll smell good like my baking.*

Pastor Mason asked her a few more questions, then stood to let her know the interview had ended.

"Thank you, sir," she said. "Good-bye."

She stepped outside to a world that seemed brighter than when she had entered. A trumpet creeper vine had made its way to the top of an elm. Its orange horns blared a bright song into the air, refracting the dull brown that had edged her life, allowing bright yellows to find their way in. The lemon verbena flourished and the mignonettes bloomed a gleaming white, overwhelming her with the beauty of life and of the city.

Beginning with one elder, word spread throughout the congregation, then throughout the community—and maybe throughout the whole world—that a Negro slave had been baptized and would, on the following Sunday morning, at the Scottish Presbyterian Church on Cedar Street, take Communion. Katy offered to receive it in her own room, but Pastor Mason insisted that she come to the Lord's Table with everyone else.

When the wondrous Sunday arrived, Katy's hands shook as she pulled on the stiff petticoat Miss Wetchee had starched for her and fumbled as she buttoned the tight, new shoes that Mr. Hendricks, the Negro cart man had found.

Tap! Tap! Tap! Miss Wetchee rapped on the back door with her walking stick. "Kay-tee!" she called, feeling a dull pain return to her chest.

"Coming, Miss Wetchee!" responded Katy, dashing downstairs through the empty kitchen and out the back door.

Though the Bruces did not necessarily buy into the

"curse of Ham" or any other Scriptures used to justify slavery, upon hearing that their slave was the one taking Communion, they were inexplicably called away.

Wetchee hobbled alongside as Katy walked up Pine Street in her light blue dress toward the big event. She kept up a commentary, calculated to boost Katy's confidence.

"What you has to 'member, Katy, is that you pleasin' the Lord. If some white folks did not have the devil in they hearts, you would not have to worry, but they do so I know why you is worried, but don't. God pleased wit' you and He been pleased wit' you a long time now. Your mother was a prayin' woman and she kept you befo' God then, so I know she worryin' God about you now. Bet God can't even walk about Zion wit'out Hannah stopping Him to ask, Is You watching over my daughter? Reverend Mason a good man. He'll stan' wit' you."

"Yes, ma'am," assented fourteen-year-old Katy, holding her hands behind her back to keep them from shaking. When they reached the Lord's house, small groups of whispering white folks drew together in tight knots, among them many she had never seen. When she and Wetchee passed, their knots drew even tighter, the ladies' fans fanned faster, the whispering fell an octave lower. Soon, the huge bell atop the steeple sounded and everyone turned to crowd in. Katy climbed the ladder to the gallery, greeting the other Negroes. Some turned their heads away, some smiled, others nodded in approval. Miss Wetchee took a seat on the short bench in back of the church, reserved for older colored who could no longer ascend the ladder to the Negro gallery.

Morning worship proceeded as usual until time for Communion. Three tables covered with pure white cloth were placed at the front of the church. Each one held a pewter tankard, four pewter beakers, and three pewter plates. At the Friday service leading up to this day, each person—including Katy—had received a coin-sized token to show that his or her heart had been prepared to receive the bread and the cup.

After the sermon, Pastor Mason read from the book of 1 Corinthians in the Holy Bible: ". . . this do in remembrance of me."

Communicants marched down the center aisle as the choir sang: ". . . love so amazing, so divine, demands my soul, my life, my all."

When the hymn ended, they took seats along the narrow tables. Each one surrendered his or her coin-sized token by placing it in a wooden tray on the table. The elder then uncovered the elements and broke the bread, giving a piece to the person sitting at the head of the table.

Katy watched from the balcony as Mr. Sam Louden took the bread, broke a morsel for himself, and passed it to the next person. This went on until all twelve had a small piece. The elder then poured wine from the tankard into a beaker and handed it to Mr. Louden, who took a sip and then passed it on. When these communicants had been served, they got up and were replaced by twelve more.

At the appointed time, Katy made her way to the cramped aisle and climbed down the ladder. Wetchee squeezed her hand as she passed. In terror, Katy walked to the nave, trying to keep her mind on God rather than on all those white folks who, on a moment's notice, might uncoil a whip and circle it in hot lashes around her trembling body.

When she reached the nave, two very tall ushers stepped in front of her with their backs to her and blocked her path. The white communicants stepped out and proceeded toward the table. After everyone had finished, Pastor Mason stood to his full six-foot height, extracted his small, rimless eyeglasses from his waistcoat, curled the stems around his ears, and raised his chin so he could see through them. His survey revealed two men in the center aisle.

The man of God stepped down from the altar and strode up the aisle. At his approach, the ushers who'd blocked Katy sheepishly stepped aside. The reverend beckoned to her, turned, and walked resolutely back down the aisle. Katy followed him to the Communion table where they sat together, while a stunned elder served the Negro communicant.

The organ stopped. A woman in the third pew, wearing a white velvet bonnet tied with wide satin ribbons and dripping with crystal-spangled plumes, fainted. Others, with mouths open, sucked in their breath, rigidly eyeing each other. All that was noble, all that was sacred, all that had been ordained by John Knox, enthroned by King James, and adopted by the great presbytery of the city of New York, had now been destroyed. A Negro had taken Communion.

When services were over, the horrified congregation withdrew in a huff from the church. Some Negroes could scarcely wait for the white folks to get out, so they could guffaw about how their master or mistress in the flock reacted to the big event.

"Katy showed 'em. They settin' thar thinkin' God belong-eth only to them," chortled one.

"The ruffles on my mistress's bonnet near 'bout dropped off when Katy handed over her token!"

"Bible say, 'Whosoever will, let him come,' but dey act like it say, 'Whosoever white, let him come.' Thank God for a man like Pastor Mason."

"Yeah," they agreed. "He God's man in dis city."

The Negroes who disapproved left as soon as they could and, when out of earshot, commented:

"Don't mean a thang to me."

"She sho' talk white."

"Forgit where she come from."

"Think she cute."

Back at the church, Katy beamed. Her eyes glowed in a special way, as though all was light and there was no darkness. Finally, she and Wetchee meandered home.

Chapter 8

A Brother in Christ

Winter 1786

*P*astor Mason's career as a pastor survived the Communion of a Negro, though not because the congregation as a whole believed that a Negro could stand equally with them before Jesus Christ, or because they believed that what he did was biblical or even right. His career survived solely because the presbytery would not remove him.

Life in the Bruce household, however, changed. The Bruce family never returned to the Scottish Presbyterian Church. They allowed Katy to continue there but moved their membership to the more conservative Wall Street Presbyterian Church, which in their view respected the order of things.

Wetchee said that somewhere along the line, white

people must have heard of Philemon and Onesimus, not that any white church taught about Philemon and Onesimus. But somewhere, they must have heard.

"Heard what? Who are they?" asked Katy one quiet winter evening, while she and Miss Wetchee sat at the Bruces' kitchen table. Two pairs of Robert's pants and one of Mr. Hoghlandt's shirts lay on the table, needing to be mended. Wetchee *loved* to tell what she had learned in the colored Bible study.

"Let me tell you," she began, wetting an end of thread with her tongue. "The 'postle Paul . . . you know who I talking 'bout?"

"The apostle Paul," answered Katy, pulling a needle through the little pants. "Jesus appeared to him along the road."

"That's him. Well, the 'postle Paul wrote this li'l book called Philemon . . . tiny book almost to the back of the Bible. Now Philemon, he was a friend to Paul. And Philemon, he had a slave name' Onesimus. Some colored peoples 'round here think they the first ones to be slaves. Slavery been 'round a long time. It's worser here, though. Anyway, Onesimus ran away. Guess he got sick o' being a slave. I know I do. 'Course I'm old now; it don' make no diff'ence. But Onesimus, he was young, he ran away. The Bible don't say how Philemon treated him . . . it just say Onesimus ran away. Well, guess what?"

"What?" asked Katy, pulling her stitch.

"He ran away from his master to be free. But by the grace o' God, he ran into Paul in Rome and became truly free. Yessir, ran right into the hands o' the 'postle

Paul. Now, I daresay that a few people could get away from Paul wit'out gettin' converted. Maybe one or two, but after Paul finished tellin' 'em 'bout Jesus, they near 'bout *had* to git converted. One thang I can say 'bout the 'postle Paul . . . he gives it to you straight. And he told Onesimus, you got to go back and make thangs right."

"Go back into slavery? After escaping?" shrieked Katy.

"Now hold on, chile. You see, once Onesimus became a Christian, Philemon was s'posed to 'cept him as an equal. Won't no more master and slave. It was up to Onesimus to right his wrong, and up to Philemon to 'cept Onesimus as a Christian brother. Paul wrote a letter to Philemon and tole him that. Paul gave the letter to Onesimus to take back home. So I guess Onesimus took it back since it's in the Bible. My pastor can read. And he read it, and that's what it say. Brothers in Christ, now that's that," she said, knotting the end of thread.

"Do you think Philemon accepted Onesimus?" asked Katy.

"Not if he was like dese white folks 'round here!"

"Then that means they won't accept me," she moaned.

"Well, baby, you equal to 'em in the most impo'tant way—spirit'ally!" emphasized Wetchee, squaring her shoulders. Their mending finished, the older woman pulled her things together and said good night.

After Miss Wetchee left, Katy snuffed the remaining embers in the fireplace and pulled her shawl closer against the cold air beginning to fill the room. She peeked in the children's room, then crept upstairs to her own room and prepared for bed.

Chapter 9

Battery Barracks in the Fort

Spring 1787

*K*aty pulled on her shawl at daybreak, tied a scarf around her head, and went out to sweep the household garbage into the gutter. Calmed by the chittering birds overhead and the faint wash of waves unfolding on shore, she turned her nose up against the smell and set about the chore. Katy liked being alone on the narrow street of low, whitewashed houses with Dutch gambrel roofs. A mauve haze blanketed the street, though soon the morning sun's bright rays would rise above the river to push away all remaining darkness.

The silence was broken by the slow clop, clop, clop of a horse's hooves over the drawling grind of cart wheels. Katy stopped sweeping and squinted toward the approaching sound. She saw Mr. Hendricks. Wearing a wide-brimmed hat, he walked alongside his cart holding the reins of his small horse, Tulip. A smile broke across Katy's face and a sense of calm overcame her. Hendricks's dark waistcoat hung open over his wide-set body, showing a brown vest over a clean white shirt. He wore dark breeches, stockings, and shoes with strings, making him a well-dressed cart man beginning his day.

At the head of New York's social class sat landowners and wealthy merchants; and just behind, eminent professionals such as clergymen like Pastor Mason and lawyers like Mr. Hamilton. The middle class consisted of shopkeepers like Massa Bruce, skilled craftsmen, and tavern keepers. Behind them were white indentureds who served a master for seven years in exchange for passage to America. At the back of the class sat Negro slaves who worked mostly as house servants or field hands on the large estates.

Hendricks, having descended from the Dutch captain of a slave ship and an African woman of the Akan people, placed somewhere in between. He inherited land but loathed farming, preferring work that allowed him to move among people. "It's the sea in my blood," he said, having lived several years aboard a ship before his father settled in New York. With Dutch deliberateness, he petitioned the licensing agent at city hall for a job suited to a man in his class, a Negro landowner with the ballot, and after two years of asking, was appointed cart man. Cart men, among other tasks, contracted with the city to haul away garbage and manure, for which they received a regular wage. When they fell behind in their work, the city called in scavenger cart men for a lesser wage. Hendricks scavenged along the docks where he was now headed.

"Good mornin', Miss Katy," he called through the frosty stillness in a low voice, traced with Dutch accents.

"Good mornin', Mr. Hendricks. It's a pleasure to see you. How are you and how are things in the Quarter?"

"Ruts in the road like buckets. No streetlights. Always afraid Tulip might break her leg," he said, patting the animal. "Other than that, fine. I ran into Miss Eliza yesterday; she sends her love. We both want to know how folks at the church are treatin' you." Miss Eliza, along with the white folks with whom she lived, had left the Cedar Street Church.

"Those still there treating me fine. Some left, you know."

"I know. But you be strong, Miss Katy. God got His hand on you. I knew your momma, Hannah, and how she trusted God."

"Yes, sir. I treasure that."

"You eatin' right?"

"Yes, sir," she answered, nervously twisting the edge of her shawl.

"You got somethin' to say, girl?"

"Yes, sir . . . since you said God got His hand on me. I want to ask you something. Mr. Hendricks . . . I want to open a school to take in poor children . . . teach 'em about Jesus, but I need a place to do it. Since you go all over the city, you seen any place I might use?"

Hendricks lowered his head in deep thought, pinching his chin between his thumb and forefinger. "A colored girl openin' a school . . . won't set too well . . . gotta

71

be some place nobody like or want . . . a place white folks won't care 'bout . . . Battery barracks. Yeah. Battery barracks at the fort; that's your place. The fire in '73 almost destroyed it, but there's enough left. You try there. Ask Mr. Bruce. Then get Pastor Mason to clear the way for you."

"Mr. Hendricks, I believe you right. The Battery barracks, what better place? My mother used to say, 'Mr. Hendricks a smart man.' She was right."

Color rose in Hendricks's tan-yellow cheeks as he smiled. "Aw, Miss Katy. Your mother didn't say that."

"Yessir, she did!"

"Battery barracks, that's your place." Hendricks patted Tulip's neck while tugging at the reins.

"She said it!" Katy insisted.

"Yeah, I'm smart all right. When I get a license to work like the white carters, then I'll be smart."

"You smart already . . . license or no."

He began to move on.

"Bye, Mr. Hendricks," Katy said while waving. "Thank you."

"You're welcome, Katy." He tipped his hat and whistled softly, as he and Tulip walked away.

The Dutch settlers, who had arrived in New York in 1628, had built a stone fort to protect themselves against Indian attacks and other dangers. It included a barracks, a church, a windmill, a maypole, a company store, and a gibbet. The fort was burned down in 1741 during the British conquest and rebuilt to provide housing for the occupying army. From it, Britain ruled the Colony until driven out by George Washington during the War when again much of the fort was destroyed. Now this illustrious place in New York history lay abandoned, in shambles.

That night before bed Katy prayed. "Lord, You far away in the heavens. Yet, You right here, holding this servant in Your all-powerful hand. Help me to be humble, Father, with holy boldness so I can get the Battery barracks at the fort to help the little children. For them, I ask Your blessing. Amen."

As the young girl prepared a special birthday breakfast for Massa, she rehearsed the question to ask afterward. The day dawned brisk and clear, with a strong winter sun giving unexpected light. The family entered the warm kitchen, greeted by sausages sizzling in the pan and the soft slap-slap of Katy flipping pancakes. The appetite-awakening aroma of fresh coffee percolating on the hearth filled the air. Mr. Bruce came first, followed by Missus with her fat-cheeked, rosy smile. She piped, "Happy birthday, honey. I put aside money from my household expenses to get everything you like."

"Smells good." A dry smile whisked across his face as he stood there savoring the sight and thumbing his suspenders. Robert and Sarah came in and took their places.

"Good morning," curtsied Katy. "Happy birthday, sir." She pulled the madam's chair out from the table.

"Katy, you've outdone yourself!"

"Thank you, ma'am," replied Katy, twinged of guilt as she noticed the roundness of the missus' hips overlying the chair's small seat.

With one long step to the other end of the table, she

deftly pulled out the other chair and nodded toward Mr. Bruce. "Sir," she said.

"Thank you, Katy. This does look delicious." Without pause, he blessed the food and reached for the sausage. Katy stood nearby ready to heap more onto their plates. The celebrant heartily ate three large sausages, eight pancakes, two eggs, and drank two cups of coffee. His wife ate half as much, and the children, sitting like little stair steps, half that, with no spills.

When they'd finished Mr. Bruce rose, placing his napkin on the table. As the children left, Katy stood twisting the edge of a napkin.

"Ah, sir . . . before you go, I would like to ask . . . ah . . . may I . . . sir, I'm sure it would please the Lord if I could help children learn what I have learned from the Bible, but I need a place to teach 'em. The Battery barracks come to mind. If it's all right with you, sir, I could clean up the barracks to use as a school. I would need Pastor Mason to help me get the barracks. Would you . . . can you . . . I mean . . . may I have your permission, sir, to ask Pastor Mason to help me in this?"

"I'll think about it," came the terse reply and he hurried from the kitchen. He knew that nothing but trouble could come from teaching Negroes. He had known it years ago when it first started. A lodge brother had freed a slave who later went to the African School, and now when the lodge brother saw him on the street, he acted like he knew as much as a white man. Mr. Bruce took comfort in seeing Negroes shuffling and dancing at the Amsterdam Market, and he occasionally tossed a sixteenth cent at them to humor himself. This girl had too much spunk for him. Too bold.

At the same time, his son, Robert, would soon reach the age when a boy started sowing his wild oats, and he did not want the boy to get any ideas about sowing them with Katy. He didn't want any yellow no-names in his house or his family. Besides, the children were reaching the age where they could help the missus, so Katy could go. He'd gotten his money's worth, and he wasn't inclined to take care of her in her old age, anyway. So maybe, if Mason got her a place in the barracks, he could wash his hands of her. Her mother baked well. She could too. In addition, he would take Mrs. Graham up on the offer she'd made to have Katy work for her two hours each day.

After Mr. Bruce thought about these things, he returned to the kitchen and addressed Katy, "Since you have extra time to be thinking of a school, you can do more to earn your keep around here. Starting tomorrow, you can bake cheese tarts to sell to my customers. After you finish that, you will work two hours each day, Monday through Friday, for Mrs. Graham, doing whatever she says to do."

"Yes, sir," she replied, lowering her eyes to hide her tears.

"My wife will see that you have what you need for the tarts." With that, he left the room. Katy's heart sank. Her stalwart knees buckled beneath her. She collapsed on a chair and cradled her head in her folded arms on the rough table. *How can I do all this?* After a moment, she resolved to get up and clear the table, wash things, put them away, and pray to God for help. As she swept the floor, a calmness overcame her. *I will do it as unto the Lord. My being a slave makes the money his. But I'ma ask if I can sell at Pinkster, and that money will be mine.* By the time Katy snuffed out her candle that night, her worries had faded away.

The next day, Missus gave her several pence to get the milk, lemon, eggs, and almonds. Though Mrs. Bruce told her how to make the tarts, Katy recounted, step-by-step, how Momma had prepared them. Make short crust pastry. Cut. Prick bottom of shell. Chop almonds. Scald milk and strain through cheesecloth. Beat eggs a bit, not too much. Add sugar a little at a time. Grate lemon rind, add pinch of salt. Bake.

Katy Williams found that she baked with ease, and her spirits rose like yeast-laced dough when she removed the golden brown tarts from the oven. She set them out on the large pewter plate that Missus kept high in the cupboard for special occasions—none of which Katy could recall—and left to make her deliveries. When she returned, the tarts had vanished. Missus told her later that they needed more lemon.

The young girl toiled on her knees, scrubbing the fireplace the next day, when Massa entered the kitchen to taste the second sample batch. Grimy and smeared with soot, she rose to face him. After several nibbles a ring of satisfaction covered his countenance.

"Very good, Katy," he said, wiping his mouth with the napkin that had covered the tarts. "Bake five dozen and bring them to the store. Save a dozen to take with you when you make your deliveries and bring the money to me. Meanwhile, don't fall behind on your chores.

And, yes," he added, "you have my permission to talk to Pastor Mason."

"Thank you, sir." She curtseyed and returned merrily to scrubbing soot.

Three days later, Katy found herself sitting opposite Pastor Mason in his small, sun-filled study. Katy sat self-consciously in a wing chair and avoided the white man's eyes. She looked instead at his desk, strewn with texts and papers surrounding a tea-stained cup.

"How can I help you?" he asked, then leaned back and listened to all she had to say. When Katy had finished, Pastor Mason turned his face to the window and let his thoughts take him back to Scotland. He remembered the shortened winter day when he had responded to a knock on the church's side door and encountered a toil-worn cotter from the Highlands.

"Fiere," said the Highlander. "I would be well pleased hae ye a sack o' feed fo' ma sheep." The fiercely independent Highlanders normally viewed people like the young pastor as soft, cowardly town dwellers. Every so often, a clan would emerge from the glens to plunder Lowland homes until the town dwellers subdued them with a show of force. Although the English and the English-speaking Scots had great contempt for the raucous Highlanders, for the most part they were looked upon as honest, hard-working people. But that was *auld lang syne*. The good pastor's thoughts returned to the request at hand.

"If this is what she wants, she should be free," he murmured, more to himself than to her, but audibly, so that she heard. The girl stood straight up like a whale breaking the waters and looked toward the window to see to whom he was talking. When the reverend turned his head toward her, she jumped back, dipping deep in a penitent curtsey, and returned to her chair.

"I . . . I'm sorry, Pastor Mason, I didn't mean to jump like that. I didn't mean to startle you, sir. I'm awfully sorry."

"Never mind, Katy," he said, waving his hand as though to dismiss her curtsey. "It was just a thought. You may go on with your plan to clear the Battery barracks. I'll talk with Mayor Duane." Katy raised her bright, brown eyes, stood up, and dared to look full in this white man's kindly face. Little folds of flesh fell gently around the minister's soft, gray eyes, so different from the cold, steely orbs in the face of Massa Bruce. His brushed back sandy brown and white hair accentuated his high forehead.

"Thank you, sir. I thank you so much. I thank God for the kindness you have showed me."

"The Lord's work is the Lord's work. I'll help wherever I can," he replied as he reached for his spectacles. "Good day."

"Good day, sir." The young believer turned to leave, holding her arms straight down, clenching her body, to keep it from galloping full out. "Hallelujah! Jump for joy! My God is real!" Freedom may have been just a thought to the pastor, but to Katy it was a planted seed, already sprouting. She hopped and skipped all the way home, but instead of going in, went next door where she found Miss Wetchee in the backyard cleaning candleholders.

"Miss Wetchee, Miss Wetchee!" she called, breathless and sweating. "Guess what Pastor said!"

"Slow down, chile! Catch yo' breath! Lorda mercy!" Wetchee set down the candleholder, picked up her folded penny sheet, and started fanning. "Whew. Cain't take too much 'citement no more."

"Pardon me!" The young woman paused and waited a second. "Can I tell you now?"

"Yes, chile, tell me now 'fo' you bust."

"I went to Pastor Mason today about using the Battery barracks and he said . . . he looked out of the window and said under his breath . . . like to himself he said . . ."

"Well, what did he say?"

Katy covered her mouth with her hands. The thought glowed in her mind like a candle in the dark. Tears began to form in her eyes.

"He said . . . he said . . . real quietlike . . . 'if this is what she wants, she should be free.'"

Katy fell into Wetchee's lap like a toddler taking its first steps. Wetchee raised her arms and shouted, "Praise God! Hallelujah! Lorda mercy! Thank You, Jesus." And her feet started stomping the ground, unchecked by the girl sprawled across her lap. Finally Wetchee jumped up shouting, sending Katy rolling onto the ground. "What would old Philemon think about that?" Wetchee tripped and fell on Katy, so that when the mistresses Hoghlandt and Bruce heard the commotion and came to their respective back doors, each woman found her chattel rolling on the ground crying and laughing.

Katy Williams stood at the tip of Manhattan Island and surveyed the abandoned fort. Only the west wall remained, hugged by the few stone barracks. Beyond lay a weeded patch where colonial gentlemen had once played the bowls but which now had become a final resting place for five patriots killed during the War. Broken muskets, rusted tin pots, ripped breeches, and dried-out buckskin lay strewn about, layered by seven years of dead leaves and the empty shell casings of hickory nuts. Katy peeled a brittle, flattened backpack from the ground . . . and so the cleanup began.

Chapter 10

Fiery Darts

Fall 1787

*T*ime permitting, Katy was able to work an hour or so each day at the Battery barracks. She reckoned she might have a space cleared before Pinkster, the African holiday in July. After that, she would figure out how to heat it in the winter. By that time, she should have her freedom and be able to move in. Mr. Bruce now had her getting up before dawn baking goods for him to sell in his store: orange pumpkin bread in the fall, cherry-studded cookies at Christmas, white snowball cakes for New Year's, and for Easter, hot cross buns. In between, she baked lemon tarts, muffins, biscuits, wedding cakes, christening cakes, and lazybones cakes with maple cream syrup. At night, her arms ached and for all she knew, her straw mattress was a feather bed. When Katy added up her chores, they totaled a fine sum. *Thank God, Sarah, Robert, and the baby are growing up spending more time with Missus and with their friends. They don't need me as much,* she thought, tossing more debris on the pile.

The next morning Katy was tired even before she had begun, but she squared herself to the task and worked until the sun hung low over Bowling Green. Soreness skewed across her shoulders, and she sat down on the grass to rest when a familiar voice called from a nearby clump of trees.

"Hey there! Is that you, Katy?" Katy stood, saw Miss Eliza emerging from the woods, and advanced to greet her.

"Miss Eliza! God bless you!" Katy embraced the kind woman who had helped her after her mother was sold.

"How you been, Katy? You still wit' the Bruces?" Miss Eliza asked, seeming detached and looking more frail and stooped than Katy remembered. Several stains spotted her faded, brown dress.

"Yes, ma'am. I'm baking cakes for Massa to sell in his store. Folks enjoy my cakes, and I like baking 'em. Where you working now?"

"Around. Why you working so hard?" Katy sat back down and Miss Eliza joined her on the grassy knoll.

"I want to open a school."

"What on earth far?" she replied, her voice rising.

Katy turned to her, surprised at her tone. "So I can teach poor children about Jesus. Train 'em, help 'em get a good start in life," she said.

"Where this school gonna be?"

"Right here, old Battery barracks, once I get it cleaned up."

"This old place? I wouldn't open no school here. 'Sides, how can you teach? When did you learn to read?" Eliza demanded in a harsh voice that startled Katy. The girl naturally approached life with a make-the-best-of-it attitude and accepted everything about herself except the fact that she had never learned to read. Eliza's words stung her with shame.

With burning cheeks she mumbled, "You know Massa forbid me to learn my letters."

Seeing the effect of her remarks, Eliza pressed on, "You got any money?" She folded her arms across her chest, seeming to dare Katy to say she did.

"A little."

"You musta stole it!" Shocked, Katy did not know how to respond. She could not believe that Miss Eliza, her friend, talked to her this way. "I knew you when you wasn't nothing," she continued. "Now you talkin' 'bout openin' a school."

"Miss Eliza," Katy sniffed, as tears filled her eyes. "Why you talking to me like this? I thought you'd be happy I'm trying to make something of myself and help others."

"Must think you something you ain't. I can't stand it when Negroes think they is white. Jesus don't care nothin' 'bout you. If He did, He wouldn't let you be a slave." Katy held her tears in check.

"Lotsa people suffer, Miss Eliza, not just slaves.

Jesus loves all people."

"I know you a fool if you think that!" said Eliza, angrily standing, glaring at Katy.

"Why are you talking to me like this? I can't believe you saying these things! Why?" Katy pleaded, meeting her eyes. "Why?" Eliza sat back down as Katy squatted facing her. After a few moments, Eliza opened her mouth to speak.

"After you went to the Lord's Table, my massa say Negros gettin' too uppity." Her voice cracked. "So he put me out to pasture. Knowing my age, he didn't even try to sell me. He tol' me to get my things and get out. He gave me a few pence, then got an Irish girl to do my work for pay."

"Oh, Miss Eliza! I'm sorry," realizing what had been brewing in Eliza's cauldron. Katy reached for Eliza's hands, but she drew back.

Looking directly at Katy, Eliza said, "All because of you taking Communion, trying to be white."

"I wasn't trying to be white. I was trying to be right before God. Besides, it was Pastor Mason's idea."

"Well, if you open a school, only God knows how many Negroes—slave and free—will get kicked out from where they has worked and slaved all they lives and got nothin' to show for it but a shabby roof over they heads."

"Where did you go?"

"To the Quarter. Where else? I got a corner in a roomin' house to lay my head in exchange for helping wit' meals and cleanin' up. All kinds of people in there. It's not safe, and it's not like the white family I worked fo' and had got used to, thinkin' I would end my years with 'em." Her voice rose again, and Katy waited before she quietly spoke.

"Not meaning no disrespect, but as I remember, your white folks never treated you well. You never got enough to eat. You were always hungry."

"But I was *used* to it. And I felt safe," she spat.

"Any Negro be *safer* with a white person 'round 'em. But are they better off?"

"All I know is, I lost my position after you took Communion. If you go and open a school, how many more Negroes gonna get kicked out!" She stood again, her eyes in slits, her lips tightened across her teeth. "I come out here to get berries so my landlady can make pies. So I guess I be on my way." She turned to leave.

"Good-bye, Miss Eliza," Katy called, her shoulders drooping.

"Don't forget what I said," she tossed back, grumbling as she marched away, ". . . slave, still wet behind the ears, can't read, talkin' 'bout openin' a school, to teach Jesus of all people. I never!" Katy stood there, holding her tears until Miss Eliza disappeared down the hill into the woods. Then they poured out in a torrent. *Why would Miss Eliza want to hurt me like that?* she asked herself.

Eliza's words forced their way into her mind: . . . *a black slave girl can't read, talkin' 'bout openin' a school.*

By the time Katy composed herself, moonlight shone through a cloud-filled sky. She dipped her hands in a shallow puddle, wiped them on the underside of her white apron, and walked forlornly home.

Chapter 11

Pinkster

July 1788

*W*etchee pulled the rickety wagon slowly to keep her clean, white cloths—and the wooden planks they covered—from falling off. The wagon bumped along from downtown all the way up to Katherine Street, on the west side of Broadway, to the Pinkster field, beyond which loomed a dense forest.

"Hope don't no foxes or bears 'cide to come to Pinkster," she remarked to Katy, who walked beside her, balancing two baskets filled with ginger cakes, cheese tarts, and shortbread cookies.

"Are bears in the woods?"

"Las' year Hendrick' say he saw somethin' move back there and it won't no li'l beaver, either. Somethin' big. All that food at Pinkster gonna be smelling so good, everythin' liable to try and get some!"

Dew clung to their worn shoes as they trudged along through the sleeping city.

"Gonna be a pretty day," observed the older woman.

"Do you think I shoulda made *fufu?*" Katy asked.

"No, lotta folks already bringin' *fufu.* Africans getting used to eatin' bread now anyway 'steada *fufu.* 'Sides, your arms woulda fell off if you tried to bake any more. That is, if yo' legs woulda kept you standin' up any longer."

"How much money do you think we gon' make?"

"Massas is us'ally gen'rous to they slaves for Pinkster. So folks oughta have a good bit to spend."

When they reached the freshly mowed, open field, clusters of people had already staked claim to spaces for selling their wares. On the far right side, two men with swinging scythes ignored the butterflies whose repose they disturbed and mowed down the last patches. Facing them across the field, several men decorated a platform with loops of yellow and white daisies, and a confection of other wildflowers. In the middle, other men laid smooth planks covering them with canvas, for dancing.

"Let's set up over there," offered Katy, pointing to a chestnut tree. "'Fore long, it'll be hot and the shade will keep us cool."

"I'll be 'sleep."

"Not to dispute you, Miss Wetchee, but I know you won't want to miss anything."

"My nap neither," returned Wetchee, drawing a chuckle from Katy as they reached the tree. Katy picked a spot and dropped her baskets. "My arm's sore," she murmured, rubbing the redness where the baskets had pressed her skin. "I'm tired of this moving bakery. I want a be-still bakery."

"When I was a girl in Africa, I coulda carried both those baskets on my head. Hey! Looka yonder!"

"Who's that?" asked Katy.

"Fulani," replied Wetchee solemnly. "She out early today. Jus' act natu'al." Katy braced herself as the girl approached. Perhaps later she would feel pity for her, but now she only felt fear borne on the stenchy smell of the girl's soiled clothing and the crawly movement of the leaf fragments that dotted her hair. Katy's heart pounded when the girl turned her eyes on her and fixed them there—eyes strangely clear, like a puddle with all the mud settled on the bottom, and through which a ripple of light seemed to pass as they studied Katy. Wetchee unconsciously tightened her grip on Katy's hand until Fulani backed away, then turned and ran.

"My Jesus!" sighed Katy, wiping perspiration from her face. "Thank God she's gone!" Wetchee did not reply.

Festive stalls at the three-day celebration featured sideshows, sorcerers, dancing, and music played on the flute, tabor, pipe, fiddle, banjo, and drums. Katy liked the musical performance by whistlers. Without a single instrument, the men whistled deep, low tones, warbled high trills and quavers—Africa's earthy melody that touched Katy's heart with sadness and delight. Fast-paced songs followed to which slaves danced with high, prancing steps.

Soon people began to enter the field: older couples, younger pairs, gaggles of giggling girls, strutting boys dressed in gaudy outfits.

"Howdy, Miss Katy," a girl called.

"How do?" she responded.

"I'll be over later to get somethin' good!"

"I'll be looking for you!" called Katy.

Soon, the field filled with Africans of many nations: Angola, the Congo, Nigeria, Togo, Guinea, Senegal, Gambia, and Mali. Most of the countries Katy had never heard of; she was Mende. But she knew that the Senegalese sold the best fish stew, with a cornmeal mush they called *menue,* and *jollof* rice. From the Togo booth you could get a good *akara,* a bean paste fritter. *Moimoi,* the Nigerian bean pudding, was tasty and plentiful. And Ghanaian spicy fried bananas tickled your tongue, especially after eating their corn dumplings, called *banku.* Other booths sold traditional African foods made from roots, seeds, leaves, tendrils, greens, dried shrimp, sesame seeds, black-eyed peas, and coconut. Everyone sold *fufu.*

"I like Pinkster," Katy told Wetchee, "but sometimes it reminds me that three generations of my family have lived here in slavery."

"Hmm," answered Wetchee, who drowsed in the shade as Katy continued her thought in silence: *I am yoked to my people by skin color and slavery, but Lord willing, my life will go beyond those boundaries.*

Once in a while at Pinkster, Katy met someone from her ancestral home, like this year, maybe. The man who kept strolling by her bakery under the chestnut tree, smiling and commenting on the beauty of her display could be Mende. He would disappear for a while, only to return to buy another cake or tart, raising redness in Katy's cheeks each time. There was something about him, something she liked. He did not have the broad nose or expressive hands of an Ibo, nor the high cheekbones of a Benin. His face was not round with full lips like the Congolese she knew. He looked Mende.

"I'm glad that you enjoy my baked goods, sir. But I would not want you to get sick from 'em," she ventured, after he'd eaten four ginger cakes.

"They is so delicious, ma'am," he replied, showing his even, white teeth. "May I be so farward as to ax the cook's name who baked such delicious cakes?"

"You lookin' at her," blushed Katy as Wetchee sat up and cut him a mean stare. He saw it and left.

"He like you," warned Wetchee. "I seen him at the Methodist church but don't really know him. He ain't been there long, plus he be mostly wit' the men. But I know one thang—you ain't got time for no foolishness."

By late afternoon they all closed their stands and advanced on center field to watch the shingle dance. Dancers performed on a square, canvas-covered platform held down by a man on each corner, contorting their bodies while high-stepping with their feet and gyrating their arms and shoulders. Drummers pulsated on their drums made of hollow logs with sheepskin stretched over the end. One by one, they danced until they could dance no more. Then, to loud clapping, each withdrew until one remained. The clapping crowd drew in to watch as the sole remaining dancer spun into seeming hysteria. Soon, the crowd grew quiet and held its breath, fearing he would collapse from exhaustion. And he did. Two men quickly came to remove his shirt, which clung to him, wet with perspiration. They propped him up to raise his arms and pull off the shirt, exposing the dancer's torso and the wide, ugly scars of a white man's lash that crisscrossed his sides and back. A collective gasp ascended from the crowd. One woman vomited and several wept as two men carried the dancer off the platform. Katy and Wetchee both bowed their heads and turned away, covering their faces in horror.

Seeing his chance, the man Katy liked approached them and held an arm to each of them. Without a word, they took hold as he escorted them back to their store under the chestnut tree. Though she said nothing, Wetchee felt a sense of being cared for as she took his arm, a sense of togetherness, a feeling of ease and of not having to be strong. She felt like a woman for the first time in many years. She wondered whether Katy felt it too.

"You coming back to Pinkster tomorra?" he asked Katy when they arrived.

She looked at Wetchee, who turned her eyes away, then she looked back at him and replied, "Yes."

"I look farward to seeing you."

The next day, Katy wore the same light blue dress she had worn to talk to Pastor Mason. It was her best dress, and though she pledged not to, Katy scanned the crowds for the man she liked and hoped was Mende. He showed up soon after she arrived, buying his first cake after he had lingered so long—trying to converse with Katy following each transaction with a customer—that

Wetchee asked, "You come to buy or look?"

"Sorry, ma'am," he said, backing away, only to return one hour later.

During his visits to her itinerant bakery, Katy learned his name, John Ferguson. He had run away from the South, hidden among Indians, stowed away on several vessels, swam some, crawled some, and gone hungry many days before reaching New York barely alive, several months ago. Colored men from the John Street Methodist Church who canvassed the wharves looking for runaways found him and took him to Mrs. Peterson's boardinghouse in the Quarter, where church members cared for him until he regained his strength. He found work as a freeman, unloading cargo on the wharves.

"I gave myself the name John Ferguson."

"It suits you," smiled Katy. She thought it matched his strong hands and steady movements. She put her arms behind her back and crossed her fingers as she asked, "Do you still go to church?"

"Every Sunday," he replied with a firm nod. Relieved, Katy uncrossed her fingers.

"What's your favorite thing about Pinkster?" she asked.

"This my first time; I'm not real sure. What's your favorite?"

"The whistlers. They're starting now."

"I'd be pleased to hear 'em wit' you."

"Me too," responded Katy as she lowered her eyes. They covered the movable bakery and walked together across the field, passing Wetchee, who admonished them with a stare that said, "I's watchin'."

Katy had met a few young men before, even free-men—smart, confident, principled men who were easy to talk or laugh with. She could have settled into marriage with them. They seemed so unencumbered with slavery's ill effects. *Unlike John Ferguson in that regard.* Most escapees had endured untold abuse. *Yet, he's . . . he's so . . . nice.*

Chapter 12

Freedom

1788

Katy strode briskly through the city on her way to see Mrs. Graham, the catechism teacher, who had summoned her. Perspiration beaded her forehead. She wove through the melodies of rich voices calling, "Straa-awberries!" "Hot corn! Hot corn! Here's your lily-white corn!" Along the streets, barefoot Negro girls with cedar baskets hooked on their arms peddled strawberries and hot corn, along with sprigs of mint and radishes. Newsboys hawked papers with clamorous voices.

Passing the Broadway shops of watchmakers, book dealers, tailors, hatters, carpet sellers, confectioners, and other retailers, she saw many people: rich dandies with high hats tapping their walking sticks, gaily dressed shoppers, Negro nurses pushing baby carriages, and Negro men steadying horses at the post.

Katy stepped off the sidewalk allowing a white family—with their lips pursed and noses in the air—to pass. Then she hopped back on it and kept on stepping, remembering the time years ago when their rude behavior would have wounded her. Along an occasional fence, showy white hibiscus basked in the sun. Winds from the Hudson River lifted the odor of horses and an occasional stray pig and replaced them with a salty freshness.

There was nothing fresh about Massa Bruce's lips when they snaked into a curious smile as he told her as soon as she arrived home from making deliveries, "Get up to Mrs. Bethune's, fast. She's waiting for you!" Mrs. Bethune was Isabella Graham's daughter, with whom she now lived. Katy reached the back door, hastening up the steps to the kitchen. Seeing no one, she walked through and peeked into the parlor. There Mrs. Graham stood in a creamy buff dress. Her daughter, Mrs. Bethune, sat on the sofa. Her raven black hair was chastely pulled back into a bun. The younger woman, with a quick movement, instructed Katy to sit in the high-back wood chair a short distance from the sofa.

Though Katy had seen this room many times and marveled at the exquisite productions of Mrs. Bethune's needle, she had never actually sat on a chair to hold a conversation with Mrs. Bethune or her mother. Usually after sharing pleasantries, she cleaned the kitchen, took whatever orders they had for her, and left.

Now, aglow with excitement, the two ladies stationed themselves on the silk damask sofa. Mrs.

Bethune rang the little bell she used to call Rufus. He swept from behind the brocade drapery separating the dining room from the parlor. He was wearing highly polished black shoes from which his white-stockinged legs rose to meet black pantaloons, and a black jacket topped with a soft, white collar. Katy had never witnessed a smile so broad as the one that covered his face as he approached them, carrying a small tray draped with a dinner napkin.

"Good afternoon, ladies," he announced through the wide grin, as his white-gloved hand placed the tray on the table.

"Good afternoon, Rufus. Thank you," smiled Mrs. Bethune. Rufus nodded and withdrew. Katy relaxed, concluding from Rufus's demeanor that the impending news was not bad.

"Katy," began Mrs. Graham, "we have something for you."

"Yes, ma'am," replied Katy with curiosity.

"Through the years we have watched you. Your work ethic is admired, your cheerful disposition is envied, and your devotion to the Christian life is an inspiration to all who know you. One year ago, I offered Mr. Bruce a certain sum if he would allow you to work for me two hours a day." Katy leaned forward.

"You have worked off that sum," said Mrs. Bethune.

"Another friend," Mrs. Graham continued, "matched the sum I paid Mr. Bruce, which adds up to an amount that he accepted in return for your freedom." Katy leaned closer, her eyes widening in shock.

Mrs. Graham added, "You learned the catechism too." Gray curls encircled her face, ascending with each gust from her pleated fan. Mrs. Bethune lifted the cloth on the tray placed there by Rufus. With graceful fingers she picked up the paper as Katy sat with her mouth hanging open. After checking it, she handed the paper to Katy, whose large brown eyes blinked back heartfelt tears.

"I know you cannot read the words on this paper, Katy, but it is a pass that allows you to move freely about. If anyone asks for your papers, show this." Katy accepted the document in her trembling hand. She unfolded it and looked at the words.

"Freedom?" she questioned.

"Freedom," she smiled.

"Freedom!" she stood up. "Oh, God, freedom! Thank you! Thank you! This is the happiest day of my life! I wish my momma could see this and my daddy and all my family who I don't even know. I'm so happy. Thank you, both."

"You earned it, Katy. But I must caution you. This is simply a pass. Your freedom papers must come from Mr. Bruce. We are still pressing upon him the need to complete them," she warned.

"Thank you, thank God!" Katy clapped her hands. "I don't know what to say!"

"We understand," replied the women in unison as the girl fell back into the chair.

"Lord, thank You for letting Your face shine upon me. Thank You for Your graciousness and Your loving-kindness. I appreciate these God-fearing women and our pastor, Reverend Mason. Thank You, Jesus, for saving me, for leading these two godly women to remove slavery's weight from me." As she prayed aloud, unashamedly, her two benefactors, obviously pleased, smiled contentedly, nodding their heads up and down and touching each other's hand. "Holy Jesus! You have answered my prayers above and beyond all that I ever asked. I want to live worthy. Amen."

"Amen," they echoed and raised their heads. When their emotions abated, Mrs. Bethune asked, "How is your work progressing at the fort?"

"Well," she confessed, "I haven't worked there in a while."

"What?" gasped the two ladies.

"I been all in a tizzy, not knowing which way to turn. I was told that what I was doin' caused Negroes to lose their jobs, that slaveholders said I was goin' too far."

"Nonsense!" trilled Mrs. Graham.

"If God calls you to do something, you do it!" spoke Mrs. Bethune.

"I've hauled out most all the trash. But there's still more to be hauled out, sweeping, raking to be done in the yard, and the inside." She could not tell them that her heart bled from the wound inflicted by Miss Eliza's words.

"Now that you're free, you need a place to live!" Mrs. Graham exclaimed. "We thought you'd live in the barracks."

"I will! I'll get it ready!" Katy promised.

"You can bake for me as long as you want, Katy.

You'll be paid for your work. I couldn't possibly find anyone to replace you."

When the former slave arrived home in the fading daylight and entered the kitchen, she found the Bruce family around the table in excited chatter, which ceased when she closed the door. Missus greeted her from the table.

"Congratulations, Katy," she chirped, wringing her hands in her apron.

"Congratulations, Katy," chorused Robert and Sarah from their chairs, while James ran to her, grabbing her around her waist.

"I'm going to miss you, Katy. Where will you live now?"

"At the Battery barracks in the fort," she replied haltingly, her emotions going into a spin. At age sixteen, she didn't know whether she was being freed or turned out. She'd spent her whole life with this family, landing there as a newborn baby in her mother's arms. The thought of having a place and living there alone overwhelmed and bewildered her. Her life was falling apart like a cask without rings.

"Thank you, thank you all," she said hoarsely, forcing a smile.

"You can stay until day after tomorrow, Katy," said Mr. Bruce. "Use the time to clean up your place and move your things."

"Thank you, sir." Katy passed the family and started up the steps, her head spinning.

"Father," she heard Sarah ask, "will I have my own room in the new house?"

"I should have my own room. I'm the oldest boy!" complained Robert.

"We'll see," replied Mr. Bruce with prideful authority. When Katy heard these words, she realized that with the money they'd earned from her baking and gotten by selling *her*, the Bruce family would buy a new house. And she . . . penniless after sixteen hardworking years . . . had to clean up an abandoned army barracks so she would have a place to rest her head. Questions crowded her mind. Where would she eat? *What* would she eat? What would she wear? How could she live?

As Katy undressed for bed, she recalled the icy cold winters when she had scrubbed clothes in the wooden tub, her fingers stiffening as she hung them to dry. She recalled the sweltering summers when she'd stood at the fireplace, cooking food and praying there would be enough left after their dinner for her to eat. And, as she sank onto her hard, straw pallet, she remembered the sleepy mornings when, as a young child, she climbed high atop their feather bed to make it up. They'd sold her mother to pay a debt. Now they were selling *her!* Her face paled, her forehead grew wet with drops of perspiration. Anger squeezed her throat and fear clutched the muscles between her shoulders. Her whole body trembled.

Long after the Bruces had finished their dinner and left for a stroll, she staggered around her room, her confidence eroded. *How can this be? Am I an ox? A donkey? An animal to be raised, worked, sold?* As though to answer her questions, a still, small voice replied, *Do you want to remain a slave or do you want to be free?*

Soon darkness fell like a veil over the city, and at last she slept. When she awoke at dawn's first light, she eased out of bed, packed her meager belongings in a sack, crept down the steps—still swathed in darkness— and left to the songs of birds stirring in the trees. She turned back for one last look, then disappeared into the ebbing darkness. *I want to be free.*

Finding her way to the Battery barracks, she entered the room she had cleared, lit a candle, and fell to her knees. "Oh, God," she cried, "please help me." Praying alone in the barracks, Katy came to know the meaning of trusting God. When the candle died out, she again fell asleep on a pallet of hay, resting her head on her pitiful sack of belongings.

When she awoke sometime afterward, she felt deeply satisfied, ready to take responsibility for her own young life, just as her mother had sixteen long years ago. Shortly after daybreak, the young girl, orphaned first by slavery and now by freedom, went to work making a place to live. She swept and scoured the wonderful hearth with its stone oven, scrubbed the walls, and gathered firewood. Her mother's words came to mind: "Eat plenty fruit and nuts." Momma had taught her to pick berries in summer and gather hickory nuts in the fall. On Sundays they'd hike to the edge of town to the peach orchard behind the hospital. *I will do as you taught me, Momma.* Unfortunately, Miss Eliza's cruel words came to mind as well. Immediately she rebuked herself . . . *I won't think of it.*

Unwrapping an old cloth and removing the coin that Sim had given her five years earlier, she bought pots, pans, and ingredients to bake her first cake as a free-woman. Other items were purchased with money earned at Pinkster.

Chapter 13

Sister

Winter 1788

*E*normous amounts of wood were needed to keep Katy's oven going, much of which she gathered from the forest floor. Surrounded by towering chestnuts, slippery elms, oaks, hickory nut trees, and juniper, the Battery barracks had proven to be the perfect location for her home. Though this fallen forestry relieved her from the daily chore of chopping wood, the job from which she had not been spared was removing ashes from the hearth, which she scooped out by the bucketful and scattered back upon the forest floor.

One evening when the setting sun layered the sky with pink frosting, she removed a bucket of hot ashes. She planned to heap them over a small hole in the clearing alongside the house, where she'd placed two sweet potatoes to bake for her dinner. While in the yard she heard a noise. She'd learned how to shut out the sound of night's swaying branches and the creeping and crawling of nocturnal animals. Now, with her mind occupied by the piquant taste that potatoes baked this way would yield, she dismissed the sound and went inside to get more hot ashes.

When she stepped back outside the door, a stenchy odor filled her nostrils, and suddenly she faced a dark figure outlined by the pink and gray sky: Fulani! They stood wide-eyed, staring at each other as the girl fondled a twig. Then Fulani looked down and saw the ember-laced ashes on Katy's shovel. She drew a deep breath, wincing in fear.

"I won't hurt you," Katy assured her, slowly pointing with the shovel to the mound where the yams were buried. The girl watched as Katy walked to it and scattered the hot ashes on top. Laying down the shovel, she returned to the girl and reached out both hands to her. Fulani dropped the twig and placed her rough, trembling hands in Katy's, and Katy began to do the only thing she could think of to do. Pray.

"Lord, here stands a child who has had everything taken away from her: her family, her home, her language, foods, clothes, her self-hood; they have been taken, Lord. This poor child rummages around the city streets. She's lost, Lord. She misses her people and her place. Some of us have made ourselves used to this 'merica, Lord. But some haven't. Some need help, Lord. This child here needs help. You can see her hurtin' heart. You can see her people back home in Africa hurtin' for her.

I'm going to ask her to trust You, Lord. If she can trust You to ease the pain, she will feel much better." The girl's hands began to relax.

After a while an aroma began to fill the praying woman's nostrils. First it seemed like the sweet potatoes. But this aroma was sweeter, lighter, more soothing, divine even. She could hear the girl sniffing, sobbing. "Lord," she continued, "help this child to release her desire for home and the people she loves. Help her to put the past behind her and trust You for the future. You promised that You will be with us if we trust You, a'cept Your forgiveness for our wrongdoing, and let the past go." When the girl nodded yes, the aroma grew sweeter, softer, heavenly, as though an angel glowed around them. Then Fulani fell to her knees. Her shoulders shook as she knelt on the ground, weeping. Katy realized that the aroma she experienced was the aroma of *agape* love, the love of Jesus Christ. Fulani had given her heart to Him.

Following a bath in the cedar tub and donning fresh clothing, the girl joined with her hostess to eat the potatoes in silence. When they had finished and scattered the cold ashes, the Fulani girl looked up at Katy, and a smile began to form around her lips. Finally, from her deep, painful silence her tongue uttered one raspy word, "sister." Then she smiled, turned, and walked away. From that time onward, the fragrance of hot sweet potatoes reminded Katy of the Fulani girl, her new sister, for whom she now prayed daily.

Katy's route today would end at the Hoghlandts', where she'd see Miss Wetchee and tell her the good news. She knocked on the back door, which usually brought a loud "Halloo! Who's dere?" This time, nothing. She knocked again, calling through the screened door, "Miss Wetchee, it's me, Katy."

A girl about ten years old appeared wearing a finely spun, yellow cotton dress. Neither African nor white, without kinky hair or straight but with large pink lips, she asked, "Can I help you?"

"I'm looking for Miss Wetchee. She here?"

"Come in." The girl led her through the door into the stifling, windowless room where Wetchee lived.

What Katy saw alarmed her. Miss Wetchee lay on her cot in the darkened room.

"Can we get more air in here?" asked Katy.

"I been fanning her," the girl contended, and Katy immediately knew her position in life. Despite her high quality dress and fair skin, she cared for a slave. She was a slave; her name was Callie.

"Let's pull this cot out from the corner, closer to the door," Katy continued. The girl proved strong as they moved the cot.

"Where is your fan?" asked Katy, and the girl pointed to a stack of old penny sheets from atop the folded clothes and "linens."

"She got heart trouble, de doctor said. Won't last long. Mr. Hogla' brung me here to take care of her 'til she die and den do her work."

"You fillin' some mighty big shoes, girl. This here ain't no trash!"

"I know dat. Missus Hogla' said this slave work hard. Told me to take good care of her."

"Where you from?" asked Katy. The girl looked away. "Never mind, child, we'll talk later. You keep fannin'." Katy took Wetchee's cool, shriveled hand and leaned over to study the face that had been like a mother's to her.

"Miss Wetchee! Miss Wetchee!" she whispered, rubbing her hand to warm it. She waited until she saw Wetchee's eyelids flutter. With great effort, Wetchee whispered slowly in a hoarse voice.

"Katy! Dear Katy! I been waitin' for ya . . . Take care o' yourself . . . Katy . . . and 'member . . . you more than a slave . . . you given to God."

"Don't go, Miss Wetchee. I'm free now. I got my freedom. Don't go." Wetchee's eyelids fluttered as her lips curved in a weak smile.

"I got mine too," she whispered hoarsely. Katy clasped the other hand, and fervently rubbed them.

"Keep fannin', girl! Fan harder!"

Two days later Mr. Hoghlandt sent for Hendricks, who arrived with an empty casket atop his cart. After the regular Sunday services, Brother Williams preached a Christian funeral for Wetchee, and the mourners walked with the funeral cart as it bumped its way up Reade Street to the Negro burial ground.

Funerals at the isolated burial ground gave Negroes the liberty to behave in their own way. So after the Christian ceremony, several women draped a cloth woven with African adrinkra symbols over the casket. Some beat drums, some danced, some rattled beads, some chanted. Before the ushers lowered the casket, Katy tossed on it a handful of wildflowers, then accepted the arm of John Ferguson around her shoulder.

She had hardly seen him since Pinkster in July. So much had happened since then. She'd gotten her freedom, moved to the Battery, and told the Fulani girl about Christ's love for her. Hendricks had relayed news of Wetchee's death to John Ferguson, so he'd come to pay his respects and to invite Katy to worship with him the following Sunday. Though her countenance brightened when she saw him, she declined the invitation because of her heavy heart.

"I understand," he said, lowering his eyes in disappointment.

Chapter 14

Cakes and Cupids

April 1789

*T*he city buzzed with excitement as it prepared for General Washington's inauguration as the nation's first president. Men constructed ornamental arches in front of the federal building. Women's auxiliaries hung colorful silk banners. Church groups festooned places of worship along the parade route with floral garlands and encircled railings with evergreen. Members of the Cedar Street Church decided to honor Pastor Mason with a social following the inaugural and invite other Presbyterians expected to be in New York for the occasion. The menu included sandwiches, tongue, ham, chicken, pickled oysters, and other delicacies. Mrs. Bethune had convinced the committee that Katy should bake the pound cakes.

At dawn the fragrance of rich, buttery pound cakes suffused the air.

"Don't you drop these, you hear?" Katy warned the young man who appeared at the barracks to get the cakes. She handed him the one cake wrapped in waxed paper, covered with a clean, white cloth, and cushioned with freshly washed burlap sacks.

"I won't, Miss Katy. I'll be real careful like."

"These are for President Washington's 'naugura-tion."

"I know."

"You can't drop a single one or let a fly light on 'em."

"Yes, ma'am."

"Who's the cart man?"

"Mr. Wilkes. He right there," the young man answered, pointing across the poorly paved street.

"Well, that's all right. Some of these reckless cart men will have your cakes broke into a hundred pieces before they get 'em where they're going. He and Hendricks are the only ones I trust with my cakes. You go on now. Take that one, then come get the other two."

"Yes, ma'am."

Having finished her baking, Katy tossed her apron in the dirty-clothes bag and began freshening the room. Hendricks would arrive soon. With Miss Eliza's accusation still dogging her, Katy had felt stymied in her efforts to open her school. Now she would find out the truth. She stood at her window adjusting her crisp organdy curtains.

Hendricks approached, pulling Tulip by her reins.

Katy opened the door.

"Good afternoon, Katy."

"Good afternoon, Mr. Hendricks. How are you feeling?"

"Fine. You wanted to see me?"

"Yes. Please come in, sit down." Hendricks's wide shoulders passed through the doorway.

"Got your place fixed up nice."

"Thank you. It's coming along. I need a new table, more chairs, a few more pans. I'm going to add tarts to my line soon's I get the right pans," she said, placing a wedge of cake on a plate before him. "I want to ask you somethin'."

"Shoot."

"I heard that Negroes lost jobs after I took Communion because white folks said I went too far. Is that true?" Her voice choked getting the words out. She held her breath waiting for his reply.

"Not to my knowledge," responded Hendricks, raising his eyebrows—along with his fork—in surprise. "Delicious cake!"

"Did anyone lose their job?" She tensed, tears filling her lower lids.

"None that I know of!" He raised his hands in bewilderment at her question.

"What about Miss Eliza?"

"Eliza lost her job, yes."

"Why?" implored Katy.

"Things are changing. A lot of foreigners are coming to New York. Many folks think good jobs should go to white, not black. Irish girl got 'liza's job. Wasn't no fault of 'liza. She's just not white."

"Why did she say it was my fault . . . because I took Communion?" questioned Katy, her tears spilling out.

"It wasn't your fault. Her white folks were mad about it and took it out on her. Maybe she took it out on you, that's all. You do what you have to do. Don't let folks' problems stop you."

"Are you sure it wasn't on account of me that she lost her job?" she cried, wiping tears on her dress.

"You can't blame yourself for what these white folks do. Do you think they consider your feelings when they make their decisions? No sirree. You go on, get yourself together, and open that school. I'm countin' on you doing it."

"Yes, sir," replied Katy, blowing her nose.

"Now one more thing. Besides helping you deliver your cakes from time to time and performing other niceties, looks like I've become a messenger 'twixt you and John Ferguson. He wants you to come to the colored Methodist meeting this Sunday. Afterward, there's a dinner, followed by a special service at five o'clock." A smile replaced the young woman's troubled brow, and her worries lifted like a bluebird taking flight.

"He do? I mean, he does?"

"A colored veteran of the Revolution will be there." This set the young woman's heart to pounding. She wanted to see John Ferguson, but she also remembered something her mother had told her years ago.

When you was four years old, your daddy came to New York looking for me and you. People from the Quarter saw him. Said a man came around asking every-

body 'bout a woman named Hannah Williams from Virginie—me—who might have a child 'bout four years old—that was you, Katherine. They described his red army jacket. Words across the front read "Liberty to Slaves." He carried a rifle. I was so proud when they told me. But when the British took over New York, I searched for him everywhere, asking everybody if they had seen Gov'nor Dunmore's colored troops from Virginie. British soldiers were all around, but not your daddy. I never found him. Everybody just kind of 'spected that he musta fought on Long Island. . . .

"I'll be there by 4:30," said Katy.

Katy got dressed, taking care to smooth her light blue dress and tilt her bonnet just so. She then made her way to meet Callie, the young girl who had taken over Wetchee's work at the Hoghlandts'. Katy had become Callie's "aunt" the same as Wetchee had become Katy's years earlier. Together they walked the few blocks to John Street. Turning the corner from Broad Street, Katy caught sight of him standing outside the church in a fresh cotton shirt, greeting members as they reached the tiny whitewashed structure adjoining the main church.

John Ferguson so much brought to mind the image of her daddy. Momma had said Daddy stood yea tall— as she placed her hand above her head with her fingers straight out—and that his square build suited his agile movements and forceful manner of speaking. Not to mention his dazzling smile. Back in Virginia, everyone took for granted that Tom and Hannah Williams would own land and have children, living as best a colored family could. However, escaping Virginia separately, they had not again found each other, and Katherine held freedom's baton alone. Here stood the man her heart told her would carry the baton with her.

"Miss Williams, I do not have words to tell you how lovely you look this evening!" John Ferguson bowed with a flourish as Callie snickered and walked on ahead. "I wager that there ain't a lily in the field as lovely as you." Katy smiled, flushed, lowered her head, and held out her hand to him. "Yo' bonnet is downright fetchin'," he continued, "and yo' smile is as bright as a rose of Sharon."

"Good evening, Brother John. Thank you," she responded to his compliments. "How are you?"

"Wonderful, jus' wonderful. Is you ready to go in?" He took her hand and placed it on his forearm.

"Yes, I'm ready," she blushed and tucked her hand through his arm, which he held close to his body so she would have to get close to him. *My hands so rough*, she moaned to herself, *and I have no gloves*. They went in, with John stopping to introduce her to his friends.

"Pleased to make yo' acquaintance," said George, offering his huge hand, which Katy attempted to shake. "John's told me a lot about you."

"The pleasure is mine," replied Katy.

One woman with curly eyelashes hugged Katy and declared, "I knew your mother, Hannah, a God-fearin' woman."

"Thank you, ma'am," she replied, flashing her rose-of-Sharon smile. They soon settled down, her skirt flaring across the third-row bench as she looked around. Despite the unadorned plank-wood walls and scant furnishings, the twenty or so people attending had displayed such a friendly, reverent demeanor that the place felt comfortable, like the house of the Lord should.

However, the flaring skirt kept John Ferguson farther away from Katy than he wanted to be. Therefore, he eased his hand toward her until, from the corner of her eye, she saw it. Then he turned it palm up like a nest awaiting the arrival of its lovebird. After a questioning glance, she landed her hand therein. He smiled, squeezed it, and with his head still bowed, and still listening to the pastor's prayer, uttered, "A-men."

After prayer and hymns, Mr. Lamb, a veteran from Stoney Point, New York, was introduced. It was explained that the Colonies had lost a fort there to the British in '77 and had appointed General Wayne to regain it. Several months went by with no success. In the meantime, General Wayne had learned about a Mr. Lamb who owned a nearby farm and regularly visited the fort to sell fresh vegetables to the British. He decided to secretly send for Mr. Lamb and ask him to spy for the Americans.

Mr. Lamb came forward looking like anything but a farmer—but somewhat like a spy—in a double-breasted vest with turned-back lapels at the chest, showing the frill of a white shirt at the opening. He did not wear a jacket. His large, rough hands hung from his shirtsleeves beside calf-length breeches that went down into his old, black, shined-up boots. He spoke in a strong voice that belied his lean frame. "I went to the fort most ever' week selling my veg'tables to the Brits: sweet corn, ripe red tomatoes. I been a farmer all my life . . . a good one . . .

blend my own fertilizer. Strawberries. My son and daughter, they pick the tomatoes ever' morning. Handle 'em careful-like, pack 'em so's they stay nice. Gen'l Wayne wanted me to find out the plan of the fort, and I found it out too." The congregation listened spellbound as he told how on the night of July 15, 1776, the Americans attacked the fort and captured it, using Mr. Lamb's description of the layout. "See this here shirt and vest I got on?" he asked, fluffing the frilly cuffs around his wrist. The small gathering nodded their heads in unison.

"Yes, sir," said one.

"Fine shirt and vest," offered another.

"Noticed it soon's you come in," remarked an older gentleman.

He continued, "I fought hard like a man and beat the Brits. But when my wife tol' me I had to wear this here outfit, I couldn't hold my ground."

The women laughed and nodded in approval, saying, "It look good," while the men laughed and nodded in understanding, saying, "We know."

The veteran went on. "After we took Stoney Point, the state of New York started 'listing Negroes in the Colonial army, but we wasn't 'listed, and the Negroes who fought on Long Island wasn't." Katy moved to the edge of the bench and leaned forward. "Many Negroes fell in the Battle of Long Island in '76. The British landed a force twenty-thousand strong—Brits and Germans —at Sandy Hook and Gravesend Cove to take Brooklyn Heights, hoping to get New York City. Many an African —slave and free—got kilt before the 'merican forces retreated across the river to New York."

Katy knew that the Colonists had lost the battle of Long Island and that her daddy probably numbered among the victorious British. She scarcely could contain herself until he finished so she could approach him. When the talk ended, she led the group that rushed to the veteran, forgetting that Mr. Lamb and her father had fought on opposite sides, and asked whether he knew anything about the colored soldiers from Virginia who'd fought with the British on Long Island.

"Yeah," he replied. "I knows that they was *shootin'* at me."

The group laughed. Katy forced a smile, trying to hide her disappointment. *My daddy, a Negro slave, fought with the British, and this veteran, a Negro slave, fought with the Americans, and it wasn't either one of their war. Yet, both were drawn in by the promise of freedom.*

Later that evening as they strolled home, John asked, "Why did you ask that veteran about the battle of Long Island? You got real quiet after that."

"My daddy fought there."

"The 'merican side?"

"Brit."

"So his side won," added John.

"I know. I only wish I had seen him."

"How do you know he served there?" And she repeated the story that her mother had told her about her daddy coming to New York when Katherine was but a child of four.

She started sobbing. "We never found him." The hurt she had felt so long began to pour out. "We figure he lost his life on Long Island. I never saw him, never knew him."

"I'm sorry, Katy." John stopped and turned to her.

"It wasn't his war, John." She fell against his chest in sorrow when he touched her waist.

"I always hoped, 'Maybe he's alive! Maybe he survived! Lord, let him be alive somewhere!' But it was only a hope. I know now that he died on Long Island. So close. It hurts so bad."

"There now," John comforted her, patting her back. He found a clean cloth in his pocket and gave it to her, holding her close, letting her cry.

"I hope you not sorry I brung you."

"Oh, no," she sniffed. "I had to face it one day." She laid her head against him, cherishing the sense of feeling cared for.

"You all right?" he asked when she became quiet.

"Yes," she replied, closing the album of memories of her father. The time had come to let go. Also, something new was happening. She realized how John's nearness aroused her womanly feelings. Lifting her head, she moved away slightly. But he took her hand and they resumed their stroll.

"Thank you, John," she said. He squeezed her hand in reply. After a while she asked him, "Did you ever see your daddy?"

"He was killed by a horse that Massa give him to tame. He loved horses. Said he had never seen one in the homeland. It hurt a long time, but I 'ventually got over it."

"Do you ride horses?"

"I hate 'em. . . . But I like you, Miss Katy Williams."

"I think a lot of you too, John Ferguson."

"There is one thing I been wanting to ask you, if you don' mind."

"Not at all."

"Not at all," he mimicked kindly. "Dat's what I wanted to ask. How did you learn to speak so proper? If you don' mind my asking."

"I learned by imitating the Sunday school teacher, Mrs. Graham, who taught at my church. I found I liked using her words, especially to speak the language of God." A burning blush and a smile covered her face.

"Oh," he said. But his mind was on the language of love.

Throughout the spring and summer, Katy attended the evening service at the Methodist meeting, bringing Callie and wearing her downright fetchin' bonnet and her rose-of-Sharon smile.

Callie had grown up in the Quarter since the age of two. Before that time, she lived with her mother and father, both white. But near the time when Callie started toddling, her reddish-blonde hair began to crinkle. Her lips, always full, seemed to grow fuller and her nostrils flared in such a way as to leave no doubt that someone in her parents' line had had Negro features. Each parent blamed the other. Her father finally concluded that he didn't want a woman with a Negro taint and walked out. Left with the defective child, Callie's mother asserted that she would not allow her family name to be besmirched, so she gave the child to her maid, Luann, and returned to her home in Boston.

Twice a year, the week before Christmas and on the child's birthday, a package from Boston addressed to Luann Hocking arrived at the post office. It contained a bonnet, petticoat, dress, stockings, and shoes for the girl. The clothes were not made from Negro cloth but quality homespun cotton, and the shoes were new. Tucked in the toe of one shoe would be a plain cloth from which fell an English guinea, worth five dollars. Luann had enough sense not to tell everyone about the money, knowing that not another package would reach her hands if folk knew it contained money. What did a Negro need money for? And if some folks in the Quarter knew she had money, they'd want to borrow it. So Luann had Pastor Williams change the guinea into shillings, which she spent almost one at a time, some going to the Manumission Society, which ran the African Free School where Callie learned her letters.

Unfortunately, Callie's schooling, light skin, and nice outfits created jealousy among malcontents in the Quarter. One day as Callie returned from school, they attacked her, ripping her dress to shreds and hiding her shoes in the bushes. Though terribly shaken up, Callie was not hurt. Following this incident, however, Luann decided to send her out of the Quarter to do live-in work, and Wetchee had asked the Hoghlandts to hire the child, convincing them that she would be a hard worker and a loyal servant.

Katy had told Callie about Jesus Christ and how He had died for her sins. Callie accepted Christ's forgiveness for herself and forgave her parents for abandoning her. She was a contented child.

One fall day after church, Katy and John sauntered along Cross Street under a canopy of red and yellow leaves. Callie and one of the young boys who sought her walked behind. With the stores closed and the streets mostly deserted, only the occasional whistling of a meadowlark displaced the Sunday quietness.

"A nice sermon," spoke John.

"I enjoyed it," responded Katy, feeling embarrassed that her heart should be pounding so. Suddenly, when they reached the corner of Cedar Street, someone leapt from behind the Presbyterian church. The person jumped in front of Katy and looked deeply into her eyes. Katy soon recognized the face—Fulani. But her hair had been combed, her clothes washed. John Ferguson, to Katy's astonishment, lifted his hat and retrieved a small package wrapped in brown paper from atop his head.

"This was going to be a surprise for you, Katy. I had it hid at the chu'ch. It's hard candy. But, if you don't mind, I will give it to dis here girl."

"I don't mind," she replied and watched as he gave it to the girl whose cheeks cracked slowly into a smile. Katy smiled back, and the girl took it and left.

"Thanks for the candy I didn't get," teased Katy. "I didn't know that you had such a tender spot." John Ferguson didn't say anything for a while.

Haltingly he confessed, "I has a chile," casting his eyes toward her to see her reaction.

"You do!" She stopped and faced him.

"I do. Her I lef' behind when I run away. But she be all right. . . . Her . . . mudder was called up to the big house and she taken the chile wit' her. Massa took my family from me. He cut 'em off from me and he cut me off from them. He took 'em right out of my cabin. I built that cabin wit' my own hands." John Ferguson stretched out his palms. "And there was nothin' I could do about it. Nothin'," he sighed with resignation. "So I left. I woulda killed him if I had stayed." He took tense, deep breaths, and Katy tensed as well, feeling his distress. But soon her heart lifted, and she eased her hand next to his. He grasped it, held tightly, and they continued to walk.

"John, I want to tell you about my dream."

"All right."

"I plan to open a school for children so they can hear the Gospel and learn to trust Jesus, make something out o' their lives." For a long time John did not reply.

"Anything else?" he finally asked.

"Yes, there is something else. A be-still bakery."

"A what?"

"I travel the city delivering baked goods. I want a be-still bakery where people come to get their baked goods."

"You got a lotta dreams, Katy." They walked along in silence until John said, "I bet you need he'p in making 'em come true."

"My help comes from the Lord."

"I mean . . . like a real person. Someone down here."

"Callie's going to help me."

"I mean . . . someone to do . . . the men's work."

"That would be very nice," Katy smiled, ". . . a Christian man."

"Maybe you lookin' at one." Their shoulders touched, causing a flutter in her heart, and she glanced at him. He looked at her, both feeling something toward each other.

He could see on first glance that this was the kind of woman he wanted, strong like him, not puny but with a square build and a serious mind. Not like the fast, silly girls where he came from. His wife had been like this girl, but she was not his to keep. He wanted a woman whose caress only he knew, and of whose love he could be sure. No telling who might be laying with his woman in the big house. Katy was easy on the eye too. Not beautiful but rosy cheeked, with bright, smiling eyes and full lips. Cheerful but no foolishness about her. A good cook too. Having left his own child behind, he could fill the ache in his heart by helping her care for the throwaway city children she seemed drawn to. And, if they ever had children of their own, so much the better. Personally, he could do without the white ones, but slowly he began to see them as she did—as God's children. This woman's heart was so pure that anyone could talk to her without fear of judgment. Better not be too many men, though. Her words were fancy and proper, but loving. She understood when he looked frequently over his shoulder. She comforted him and told him how strong his arms were and how brave he was to have escaped slavery. He began to picture himself as an angler bringing in his catch.

She asked, "What's your dream, John?"

"I like workin' on the dock. The air smell like fresh-cut pine, 'cept when it's filled with the smell o' tar and pitch. Hammers is all day banging on the pilings. Seamen from all over the world is around. Men building ships. I like the going back and forth. Unload one ship and fill 'er up with something else, then she's gone, and in comes another. I'd like to stay on.'"

After that, they walked downtown to look at Katy's home and the room she had chosen for the school. Along the way they passed other Sunday strollers who basked in the last days of Indian summer.

"You know, Katy, winter is coming and you gonna need firewood. 'Sides, how you gonna get down to Whitehall Street through the snow carrying your cakes? Wolves gonna be howling from them trees over yonder, and you gonna be scared out here by yourself. Have you ever thought about those things?" asked John.

"Yes, I've thought about them."

"Well—what is you gonna do?"

"I don't rightly know." Her pulse quickened as her mind rehearsed how to casually say yes should he ask to marry her. It had been all Katy thought of since Pinkster. All week she anticipated their Sunday meetings and found herself more than once sauntering past the wharf at South Street near the Fulton Market where he worked, hoping to catch a glimpse of him.

"I'd be happy to he'p you out."

"Oh, John, how kind," she smiled as she squeezed his hand. In her mind she pictured him coming up the hill to the Battery barracks, tired from a long day's labor. She'd have a hot meal ready for him and water for his bath.

"Do you want me to or not?" he asked.

"Of course I want you to. You know that." They reached an isolated area where scarlet leaves adorned the trees. He stopped and turned to face her. He took her hands in his.

"What I'm saying, Katy, is I love you and I want to marry you." Her eyes widened in awe. As much as she had dreamed of this moment, it caught her by surprise. John stared at her, waiting for her to speak, but her mouth wouldn't move. Her eyes glowed like the sun illuminating distant hills, but her mouth would not move. He didn't know what else to say but knew he needed to say something.

"Will you marry me?" he stuttered, almost shouting. Katy spoke, "Oh yes! Yes!"

The question remained as to what kind of wedding ceremony to have, which Katy discussed with Luann one afternoon as they shopped. John felt at home in the Methodist church and Katy felt at home with the Presbyterians. Though confident that Pastor Mason would perform the ceremony, she did not want to ask. Yet, he might feel offended if the ceremony were held in the Methodist church. On the other hand, if Pastor Williams married them, she would feel a debt to the Methodists that she did not want. Her interests were too closely tied to her home church.

"Why don't you get married in the Quarter?" suggested Luann, selecting a tomato.

"Where 'bouts in the Quarter?"

"You could get married in Mrs. Peterson's boardinghouse. It's the biggest house in the Quarter. You could have the reception right there. She wouldn't mind a-tall."

"I don't want any drinking," asserted Katy, looking up from a barrel of pickled meat.

"Mrs. Peterson don't allow it in her house. She's a godly woman, like you."

"Thank you, Luann. I take that as a compliment."

"She don't allow drinking *or* gambling."

"I love my people," continued Katy, "but too many are hurtin' and they cause trouble for themselves and others. They need Jesus so they can forgive and be healed."

"Amen," reflected Luann.

"I'll ask John if Pastor Williams will perform the ceremony at Mrs. Peterson's."

"What about the part that says ''til death do they part'?" asked Luann somberly.

"What about it?"

"They don't say that in colored marriages 'cause them massas can break 'em apart any time they want to," she answered. Her words cut Katy like the spikes on a whip.

"But we're free!" she protested, dropping her packet of butter.

"I hope that's enough," said Luann, as scenes flickered through her mind . . . the man she'd seen snatched away by slave catchers . . . Callie's parents separating.

"You're right, though. Slavery doesn't leave anything untouched, does it?"

When no one spoke, Katy answered her own question: "I reckon not."

"Pastor Williams will perform the ceremony. He only charge twenty-five cents." They finished their shopping and went to their homes.

On the sunny October day set for the wedding, Luann and Callie went to the boardinghouse in early morning to prepare candles, hang festive tendrils of red ribbon, set out pots of marigolds and chrysanthemums, and sprinkle the porch with fragrant needles of pine. Inside, boarders laid out a mouthwatering feast including roasted chicken, sliced beets, buttered cornbread, and squash. None of the women felt capable of baking a wedding cake for Katy, so they served cookies decorated with smooth, white icing and French apple pies.

When all was ready, Katy entered the room in a high-waisted white muslin dress with fitted sleeves that softened the lines of her figure. The wide bodice swung low, showing off her smooth brown skin and emphasizing her perfect bustline. The ruffle at the bottom of the full-skirted dress stopped exactly one inch above the floor and stayed clean.

At two that afternoon, Katherine Williams, daughter of Tom and Hannah Williams, who'd been born on a schooner as her mother fled to New York from slavery in Virginia and who was now surrounded by friends, including Mrs. Peterson and her boarders, was given away by Mr. Hendricks. She became Mrs. John Ferguson.

"I now pronounce you husband and wife," said Pastor Williams of the John Street Methodist Church.

Chapter 15

Mrs. Ferguson, School Mistress

1789–1790

The dried cornstalks, red chrysanthemums, golden marigolds, and red ribbons dangling from Hendricks's cart bounced gaily to a stop. John Ferguson released his bride's hand and jumped off the cart with a smile. She smiled back. Cradling her in his arms, he carried her across the threshold of the Battery barracks and gently let her down. The door closed as they waved good-byes to their friend Hendricks. Before the wooden latch fell, they turned to each other.

"I have never been happier than I am at this moment!" she cooed.

"Mrs. Ferguson, you have made me the happies' man in the world!"

Warm breezes stirred the fragrances of boiling apples,

baking breads, and hickory wood burning on the hearth. Only an occasional high wind from the river ruffled the Fergusons' cozy nest. The husband chopped wood and piled it high against the barracks, ready for his wife's oven. The wife kept the mound of biscuits high on the sideboard, ready for her husband's appetite. On Sunday mornings they attended the Methodist church—to which Mrs. Ferguson resigned herself—and afterwards held Sunday school classes in their home. She visited Mrs. Peterson monthly for tea and conversation. John's friend George, from the docks, visited him and ate as though to fill the hold of a clipper ship. Her giftedness as a baker had been sealed, and she no longer had to sell cakes in the streets. She received enough orders and had only to deliver them.

One Sunday afternoon John made his way from the fort to Whitehall Street and turned right, away from Broadway toward the East River wharves. In the sooty recess of an abandoned red brick building, he spotted a gray-brown mass of rags with shoes sticking out, from which arose several low snores. A tap of his toe against the mass revealed one of several bands of youngsters who roamed the streets, living by begging and thievery, sleeping in areaways and under doorsteps, in old crates and hogsheads, never seeing the inside of a school.

"Hey!" he called out. "Y'all want somethin' to eat?" The living pile began to undulate and separate, giving John a sick feeling in the pit of his stomach.

"You got somethin'?" a sleepy voice attempting to sound gruff replied from the ragged bunch.

"My wife got hot biscuits waitin' for you. Come wit'

132

me." John turned to lead the way. The ragged mass separated into four boys, one of whom pulled a smaller child by the hand, making five. They trailed along behind John without a word until they passed through a bog not far from the barracks. Then the leader called out, "Cranberries!" The four larger children ran to the bush as fast as they could, pulled the red fruit with their grimy hands, and stuffed them in their mouths like hungry bears.

"Oww!" cried one whose small foot sank in the bog. John pulled him up, then watched with sadness, remembering the nights during his escape from the South when berries such as these controlled his hunger pains. Compassion welled up in him as he envisioned himself lying on the ground with barely enough strength to reach up to the bush, devouring one berry after another until the ache in his stomach eased enough for him to grab a handful and move on. The leader gave several berries to the smaller child with him. John squatted to help them. Finally he said, "Let's go." They looked toward the leader, who got up to follow John, and they fell in behind.

Katy waited in a small barracks room near the kitchen where she'd set up an old stand with a basin, a cloth, and lye soap. Beside the stand sat a bucket of cold water to be mixed with hot water from the kettle steaming on the hearth.

"Good afternoon! Welcome!" she called as she saw the crew coming toward her. "This way! You must wash your face and hands before you eat." The leader went first. He took off his heavily soiled hat and washed his grimy face and cranberry-stained hands in the warm water. A white boy! John looked at Katy, and Katy at him; they shrugged their shoulders. Katy emptied the basin and filled it again for the next child. There were three white boys and one skinny, light-brown-skinned Negro boy named Jed. The smallest child was a girl, the leader's sister, who seemed to be mute. He washed her face and hands.

After all the children were reasonably clean, John led them to the long table and lined them along the bench. On the table Katy had laid out a stack of biscuits and five cups of water.

"I don't have any milk today. But you're welcome to put syrup on your biscuits," she offered, setting down the bowl. "It's warm."

"Thanks," they mumbled. John blessed the food and they tore into it. Afterward, Katy cleared the table and sat opposite them. She led a Bible song in her seasoned, mellow voice, told each child that Jesus loved him or her, and had them begin memorizing John 3:16:

> For God so loved the world, that he gave his only begotten Son, that whosoever believeth in him should not perish, but have everlasting life.

The children did everything they were told, obeying the firm husband and his wife to the letter. After they discussed the verse and talked awhile, reluctantly but dutifully they departed, turning back to wave at the couple who had fed them. All except Jed. He grabbed Katy's skirts and would not let go. She gave him her last ripe peach, and he stayed for four days until an aunt discovered his whereabouts and came to claim him. His parents had been jailed for being involved in a brawl.

This scene played many times during the following months, sometimes with new children, sometimes with the same children. Soon the Fergusons were asking church friends for old clothing, tin plates, and cups. Callie came to help manage the children, and John cleared out another room for those too young or sick or weak to go back out on the streets, or who simply, like Jed, did not want to go.

Most poor children who found shelter in the business district, through which John had to pass, were white. But when John left home in the afternoon to collect the waifs, he'd have as many as they could handle before he got very far beyond that district—the occasion for much prayer.

"Lord!" he cried out in anguish, "with all the suffering of our own people, would you have us take care of these white children?" *They are not white children; they are My children.*

As John and Katy's responsibilities grew, they needed more help and asked several colored leaders at the Methodist church to teach on Sunday when the children came.

"I ain't teachin' no cracker nothin'," one man maintained, seeing several white children in Katy's school. Others were too busy, and the few who came did not stay long. Having nowhere else to turn, Katy sought a meeting with Pastor Mason.

"I need teachers at my school," she stated, facing him across his desk. "Several children live with us now and others come every Sunday. I have someone to help care for them, but I also need someone to help teach. I must keep up my baking to support the school. And my husband works at the docks from sunup to sundown, supporting the household. It's all he can do to chop the wood and keep things fixed up. I've come to see if you can help me."

"Let me think about it, Katy. I'll see what I can do."

"Thank you, sir." She got up to leave but turned back, having noticed that he appeared somewhat haggard.

"Sir, if I may ask, are you feeling all right? You appear a bit pale." He seemed pleased with her concern.

"I have been a little tired, Katy. Can't go like I used to. But thank you for asking." In fact, he felt tired much of the time, and his thoughts drifted increasingly to his homeland: its Highlands and hills, thatched cottages, grand castles, and its church.

Having served on Columbia College's board of regents, Pastor Mason knew the problems facing theology students, one of which was finding places to teach what they'd learned. He decided to request that students teach at Katy's school.

However, this would have to wait. Many privates homes—occupied by leading citizens—stood near the salient angle formed by the Hudson and East Rivers, near the Battery barracks. Elegant mansions had been rebuilt nearby. Boasting sumptuous furnishings imported from Europe and impressive libraries embracing the standard works of the day, these residences required an idyllic setting; a collage of magnificent trees, fine grasses, and exquisite flora; a setting where elite society could stroll on Sunday afternoons and delight in the breathtaking view. The city now planned to convert the area around the old Battery into a public walk. Katy Ferguson would have to move.

The pastor gave her this unwelcome news but told her that once she moved and got settled, he would try again.

"I'm sorry," he concluded.

"Thank you, sir," she sighed, recalling the hour upon hour she had worked to clean up the old place, the loads of trash that Hendricks had hauled away, the rats, and, oh God, the snakes.

Katy walked slowly home as dark clouds formed in the sky. Stray snowflakes began to drift down, and she pulled her shawl snugly around her shoulders. Blankets of fluffy white moisture began to cover the grass, and people hastened to get home. Questions filled her mind. What would they do? Where would they go? How much time did they have? What about the children?

Chapter 16

The Wilderness Experience

1791–1799

*T*he wooden floorboards in the new two-and-a-half story row house they rented on Warren Street brought about much rejoicing on the part of Katy Ferguson. "God is real!" she proclaimed.

"I ain't never seen nobody so excited 'bout a flo'," complained John as he struggled past her with the straw-filled sleeping mats.

"You can't imagine how hard it was to keep dust from flying up, landing on my pots and pans and everything, John! Thank You, Jesus, for this floor! Even the baby likes it," she smiled, rubbing her tummy. She left the pile of clothing on the table and crossed the room to her husband. "Look, John, feel her! She's happy!"

"I ain't seen a speck o' dust on nothing the way you

always fussin' over the house. In addition, *he* happy," John corrected her. "I keep tellin' you, it's gonna be a boy."

"I'm glad winter set in and the ground froze before the city began work on Battery Park, so we did not have to move until spring, and I sure am happy to be here now. A wood floor! Thank You, Jesus!"

Katy awoke feeling downhearted on a day in April 1792, when morning glories closed their blossoms against a muted sky. She pulled herself up and washed her face without warming the water, hoping its coolness would rouse her. A heaviness still clung to her when she opened the door for John to peck her cheek, grab his lunch, and hurry out.

"Bye, honey, hope you wake up soon," he teased.

"I will." As she closed the door, she mentally listed the day's chores: fix breakfast for Tyro, Susie, and Jed; go over their Scripture verse; send Tyro for two buckets of water with firm instructions about not stopping to talk; show Susie how to make beds and tidy up; teach Jed for the third time how to make a fire for the oven.

She worried about Jed. He was a tall, smiling boy, gentle and affectionate but a bit slow. And the oven must be right for the christening cake she had to bake before lunch. She remembered the first time Jed came to her, with a group of scrawny white children. Immediately she and John had taken a liking to him, and she was so pleased when he found his way back. Perhaps making a fire was too difficult for him. But he would learn. John would see to that. Tyro, on the other hand, was small built with quick movements, and talkative. Susie was her right arm after Callie left in the evenings.

Katy checked her pantry supplies, stoked the hearth, and made sure the kettle would yield a full cup of water for her morning tea. She'd sat down and taken several comforting sips when a knock came at the door. *Perhaps whatever news comes will lighten my burden,* she thought, forcing a cheery "hello" to Greenie, the gardener at the Presbyterian church.

"Good morning, Miss Katy. I can't stay, but I came by to tell you because I knew you would want to know. Sit down, please," said Greenie. Katy pulled out a chair and sat.

"It's Pastor Mason." Greenie paused to give Katy time. "He died this morning."

"Oh, Jesus, Jesus!" she cried, sinking into the chair. Tears spilled from Greenie's eyes also as he got up to put his arm around Katy and pat her on her shoulder until she composed herself.

An usher allowed Mrs. Ferguson through the throngs of mourners. Black cloth draped the pulpit, organ, and galleries under lighted chandeliers. After the organist played a dirge, a procession of several hundred ministers representing the Presbyterian, Dutch Reformed, Baptist, and other churches entered the building. The coffin, draped in black cloth edged with silver, had been placed before the pulpit. On the family pew she could see Pastor Mason's widow and both his daughters, who were now married and living out of state.

From the gallery Katy heard all that was said about him: staid deportment . . . gentlemanly manners . . . very strict in family discipline . . . given to hospitality. His sermons were well studied, his delivery plain and energetic. A man of sound, strong mind, of extensive learning, and of unusually fervent piety. As a preacher, uncommonly judicious and instructive; as a pastor, singularly faithful and diligent; as a friend and companion, he displayed an assemblage of excellencies rarely found to such a degree in one person.

She listened with sadness to every word the distinguished speakers had to say. But none said, "He led a poor, colored girl to the Lord at his church, where she took her first Communion."

Pastor Mason's son, John Mitchell Mason, who had graduated from Columbia College in 1789, returned from his studies in Scotland to assume his father's duties.

Upon the birth of her first child, a pretty baby girl with cuddly cheeks and sparkling eyes whom they named Abigail, Katy's grief lessened.

"She got yo' eyes, Katy, but she got everything else from me, 'specially the mouf!"

"Such a proud daddy!" proclaimed the new mother from her new bed, which John himself had built.

Abigail renewed Katy's zest for life. She and John had found a home for an orphan girl who lived with them, and now only one other girl and two boys remained. But even with Callie's help during the day, Katy often became disillusioned by the grinding poverty of the urchins to whom she ministered: their poor manners, ungodly talk, and their habit of settling every quarrel with a fight. But even their hearts softened when they beheld Abigail, who, at three weeks, curled her tiny mouth into an engaging smile.

"See?" boasted John, dwarfing Abigail in his muscular arms. "What did I tell you? My mouf!"

One day in early June, John arrived home very excited.

"Katy, slaves in Haiti rose up and run out the French plantation owners and they black house slaves. They is coming to New York. Plus stowaways. Hundreds came in at the docks today. More coming."

"What?" asked his wife, looking up contentedly from her kneading.

"A black man named Toussaint. The white Frenchmen was so busy revolutin' that Toussaint saw a chance to run the slaves right through it. Got folks runnin' every which-a-way. Ha! Those slaves speak French. You should hear 'em, Katy."

Within days she did. A small group of Haitian Creole men and women flounced gaily up Broad Street dressed in brightly colored clothing. They seemed to float past Katy as she, pregnant again, lumbered along with a basketful of cakes on her arm and floor plans for a be-still bakery in her head. Behind them followed a very dark woman wearing a flowing white dress. She smiled and said, *"Bonjour."*

"Bone-jure," nodded Katy, and the woman seemed pleased with Katy's attempt to return her greeting in French. Still, something about these foreigners worried her.

Most of the black Haitians had served French families before the insurrection. They had stood beside their masters through its dangers, escorted them safely to departing ships, loaded their luggage, and waited on them at sea. Now in America, many of the French people, with their plantations gone and no steady income, released former slaves to fend for themselves. Those who could adjust to their new surroundings found work; those who could not became fearful and disoriented and landed in jail, or else they loitered and begged.

Stowaways wandered freely. When constables chased them, they darted into alleys and small passageways that led up to the Quarter, or into the forests beyond Chambers Street where they disappeared. Constables jailed captured vagrants in the Bridewell. However, over a period of time, many escaped north, taking local slaves with them.

The whole picture made Katy nervous, partly because her baby seemed to recoil in her womb each time she passed a foreigner and partly because of the stricken expression on white faces. The black uprising struck fear in their hearts, arousing hostility and bitter prejudice. As summer progressed they seemed to resent Negroes, even those whom they had known for years.

While John and Katy prayed for the refugees, they also braced themselves for the retribution to which white fear always gave birth. They did not have to wait long. New York passed laws for the capture of fugitive slaves. Poor whites went after them in zealous pursuit. All over the city, mean white men skulked, wearing buckskins and beards . . . eyeing every Negro who passed . . . stalking . . . waiting for a catch. Ever anxious to display the superior position of their race, they often demanded that free Negroes such as Katy, suffering extreme humiliation, produce the papers she had so timely received from the Bethunes.

Remembering that France had aided America in its war against Britain, the local government gave land, farms, tools, free transportation, and provisions to help white Frenchmen start new lives. By November, they had begun to blend into the population, and Katy even began receiving orders from one for Christmas baking.

Winter passed, and when daffodils began to peek through the soil in whitewashed wooden boxes beside the front door, Katy stopped taking orders, baking only for regular customers who could arrange for a pickup. Her second child was now due.

"You gonna have a sister," she announced to Abigail one morning as the child crawled across her and John in their bed, having left her own.

"A *brother*, Abigail. Listen to your daddy, girl!" corrected John as Abigail snuggled between. But later, he whispered in a strange tone, "Katy, I really wanted a boy so he could take care of you after I'm gone."

"What on earth are you talking about? Why would you upset me with that kind of talk, John Ferguson?" When he said nothing, hysteria rose in her voice. "John! What are you talking about?"

"Just a dream I had." He turned to her, cuddling her in his arms, calming her. "You know ain't nothing gonna happen to me."

The following week, from the little chair her daddy made her, Abigail cooed and gurgled while her mother figured out the day's baking needs. A knock at the door interrupted their day, and Katy opened the door to three men, led by George, John's Methodist friend who also worked at the dock.

"Good afternoon, Miss Katy. We from the dock."

"Oh, my God, no!" screamed Katy. Blood surged through her body, pounding her ears like a drum. "What? Where is John?"

"Please sit, Miss Katy." She grabbed a chair and sat, watching them expectantly.

"Some evil-smelling men stealers came looking for a Haitian. John tol' 'em he won't no Haitian. Couldn't speak no French. But dey tackled him. Six of 'em—bearded men in dark clothes. Threw him down and tied his hands behin' his back. John, he hollerin' saying he won't no Haitian, he free. But dey wouldn' listen. De boss wasn' dere to tell 'em John won't no Haitian. No white folks aroun' to tell 'em who John work for. Just Negroes. An' dey tol' us to shut up or we be nex'. Dey tied John's hands behin' his back and stood him up and tried to put chains around his ankles. What dey do dat for? John went wild. Said he wouldn' be chained. He won't no Haitian and he won't no dog and he wouldn' be chained. He kicked one of dem dumb vigil-ants as hard as he could and de vigil-ant, he went flying backward, blood a-running out his mouf and his teeth laying on th' ground. Den one pulled out his gun an' he said, 'Negroe, you wanted dead or alive, and fo' dat, we taking you back dead.' Den he started shootin'. John fell, but de vigil-ant, he kept on shootin'. 'You don't kick no white man. Ya hear? Ya hear? All you Negroes hear?' So de boss heard all de commotion and come runnin' down an' tol' dem vigil-ants to move out his way and he see they kilt John. Then he start yellin', 'You fools, you fools, you kilt my best worker!' An' dem vigil-ants they run around and snatched they ropes and chains an' run off. Ain't seem 'em since."

Katy dragged herself to their bedroom and walked to the bed that they'd slept in last night and arisen from this morning. It was now smooth and cold. Unbuttoning her dress and stepping out of it, she left it on the floor with her shoes atop, then purposefully pulled back the quilt and climbed in. It was too much to bear. She had to have something of her husband . . . if only the smell of him. So she laid her head on his pillow, pulled the quilt up around her face, and cried herself to sleep.

The widow Ferguson grieved in deep solitude on the front row of the colored section of John Street Methodist Church. On one side of her sat Callie, swaying mournfully, and on the other, Abigail, with her thumb in her mouth. Throngs of mourners filed by to hug Katy, to squeeze her hand, or simply to be there. Three deaths in five years: she'd hardly gotten over the loss of Wetchee before Pastor Mason died—now John. One moment she felt hollow and empty, like she might float away. The next moment her heavy heart pulled her down into utter darkness.

Then someone squeezed onto the pew beside her where Callie had been, disturbing the warmth. Thin, strong arms enfolded her and pulled her back.

"Katherine," murmured a voice . . . gentle, reassuring. The voice sank into Katy's consciousness. "Katherine," the old woman's voice whispered again, as Katy listened. "Katherine." Tears began to roll down her cheeks, and the thin, strong arms pulled her closer, pressing her head to their shoulder. Only one person other than her mother called her Katherine. "It'll be all right, Katherine."

"Miss Sim," sighed Katy, lifting her eyes, "you're back." And the sorrow of recent days poured itself out on Sim's shoulder.

Following the funeral, Sim walked home with Katy and Abigail, as Callie returned to the Quarter with some others.

"Where are your things?" Katy asked.

"At Mrs. Peterson's in the Quarter . . . what's left of 'em."

"Is that where you'll be staying?"

"For now. That's the first place I could get to."

"I'd be happy to have you come live with me."

Sim brightened. "I'd be honored . . . that is . . . if you can tolerate an old sinner like me."

"We'll work it out."

"I'll be on my best behavior." The women turned to each other and grasped hands, sealing their pact, then resumed walking. "How long were you and John married?"

"Seven happy years," Katy replied, smiling, remembering. The two sat up all night with her telling Sim of her love for John and of the tragic way he died. Sim told of her exploits.

"We landed in Nova Scotia and no sooner had I put my foot on the ground than I knew it weren't for me. All around was shaggy, green forest; gray, rocky shore; and cold, hard ground. Three flotillas landed when we went but the *Martha* didn't make it, lost more than a hundred people. Cap'n Winchester got sick that first winter, and I nursed him as best I could. But 'fore spring, he died and I had to move in among the Negroes. We lived in thrown-together cabins, shacks, spruce-thatched tents . . . anything we could put together."

Katy eyed her wind-leathered face. "Could you plant a crop?"

"Whites got the best land, you know. Our little patches were grim and stoney. We learned to live off the sea."

"What made you come back, Miss Sim?"

"I had found a place with a nice Negro family and worked in a mill. But land grants for us was small and hard to get, and some could not get by with just fishing. Finally, after years of fruitless negotiatin' for land, Tom Peters led more than one thousand back to Africa, to Sierra Leone. Fifteen ships, Katherine, filled with colored folks, going back home. What a sight! The older ones got on board laughing and excited, looking forward maybe to seeing their kinfolk again. Some said they never wanted to see another white face in they life. Others was plain *cold,* said they'd been shivering since they left New York. What a time! I waved good-bye for hours, watching the sails disappear, one by one. I felt so alone. Even when I got back to my room, where I lived, it seemed so empty . . . the things I had in it did not matter." She paused. "Do you 'member that guinea I gave you?"

"Yes, I don't know what I would have done without it when the Bruces let me go."

"I had several of my own and some other things. I sold most of it, enough to get me to Boston. Then I had to walk, so I sold the rest." Sim's voice cracked, and Katy reached across the table to take her hands. Sim continued.

"My momma always told me to use my light skin and my looks to get everything I could, especially from white men. Look what it got me!" Sim paused and a pained expression crossed her face.

"Awful things can happen to a colored woman alone on the road, Katherine." Tears rolled down to her trembling lips. "Sometimes, the only thing kept me going was your mother's words, 'I given her to God. She more than a slave, Sim. But she need a' earthly mother. Take her under yo' wing like I taken you under mine.' I kept seeing the hurt you suffered with Hannah gone. I kept telling myself that I was coming home to be your mother. But now I'm so wore out I need you to be mine." Sim dropped her head to the table and cried.

"There, there, Miss Sim, it'll be all right." Katy moved closer to rub her hand along Sim's back.

When Katy awoke the next morning, she knew she had to go on. She had Abigail and the children to care for, her friends, Sim, Callie, Hendricks, Luann, and George. In her heart, she also knew that Jed would come back again. John had been like a father to him. She'd seen him at the funeral, but he had gotten lost in the crush of folks. Katy also knew she would go on because there was a new life inside of her soon to be born.

But by the time February's fluffy, cold snows began to harden into ice, she knew that something was going wrong with this pregnancy. The warm promise of new life seemed to turn cold like the blocks of ice in the river. Perhaps this child sensed she would not have a father to steer her life. Perhaps she sensed what lay ahead for her mother. Only God knew why the life begun in Katy's womb would not continue. By the time the chilly March winds blew across Manhattan Island, it was over. On the day of the small funeral, Katy allowed Sim, as they shivered in the cold, to name the child Julia. Then they returned home to face a cold March of grief.

Chapter 17

The Turn of
the Century

1800–1829

As the city grew, it spread northward, and by the end of 1800, it had extended to Canal Street. Warehouses and factories replaced quiet residential areas, and newly installed oil lamps turned on at dusk, lighting main thoroughfares for the 60,000 residents.

Pastor Mitchell moved to Pine Street, staying downtown near his church. Deciding to stay uptown, Katy purchased the house she had rented on Warren Street and the one adjoining it. As she traversed the city to deliver her cakes, one of her favorite places to stop, rest, and talk with God continued to be the Cedar Street church, to which she had returned after her husband's death. Every Monday, she reached the quiet sanctuary, left her basket beside the step, and went in to kneel and pray. She marked the passing years with prayer.

Lord, I regret that my husband did not live to see the colored Methodists move from John Street to their own Zion African Methodist Church. But I appreciate the time we had. And, Lord, she added, *I'll always treasure my downright fetchin' bonnet as a memory of him.*

Her prayer included the new children she had taken in from the orphan asylum. Three years earlier, Mrs. Graham, concerned about the aftermath of a yellow fever outbreak, had asked Katy to pray for the formation of a society to help the victims. *Along with the children I already take in from the streets, Lord, I have the overflow from the orphan asylum. Please continue to touch people's hearts to share their wealth so that I can feed hungry mouths and provide warm clothing in winter.*

The yellow fever had struck the city in 1798 and again in 1803. During the first attack, despite Katy's unceasing vigil, her nurturing care, and the prayers of many, Abigail, her firstborn, succumbed. Katy wept and prayed until the Lord comforted her. And though her numbed heart had scarcely healed, she made time to comfort others and rejoin the effort to curtail the fever. Farmers stopped bringing their produce to city markets. Business was suspended; schools and churches closed. More than two thousand were buried before the siege ended.

Authorities attributed the outbreaks to polluted water. So Katy prayed for the city's water supply. *Ever since I can remember, the Collect Pond has welled forth from deep springs, the clearest water You ever put on the earth. Now with the trees that surrounded the Collect being cut down to build more houses and businesses, the water has begun to taste poorly. Sometimes I have to boil it before I can use it. But You know the situation, Lord, and I trust that You are working it out.*

She thanked God for allowing her to open a Sunday school and for sending Miss Sim to do the mending. She asked that He continue to bless it by giving her all she needed to keep going. Pastor Mitchell had promised her a space in the new church soon to be built on Murray Street. Katy wondered what people would call the new church. *We'll see what happens. It's in Your hands, Lord. You know that I got a lot more children I want to give to You.*

The years rolled by as each week—rain, snow, or shine—she stopped by the spot where her Sunday school would soon be on Murray Street. Like a griot, she could recount events by her prayers. *You've been a father and a mother to me, Lord.*

During the second yellow fever outbreak, Katy mourned anew for Abigail. She also prayed for the Negroes arrested for burning down eleven houses. Folks accused them of planning to burn down the whole city. Their arrest incited others to riot, and rioting ensued for several days before being brought under control by constables. Twenty men were convicted, including an orphan boy, Cato, she had fed many times and who had chopped wood for her on occasion.

In 1804 she prayed for Mrs. Hamilton, whose husband had been shot to death in a duel, leaving all who knew them overwhelmed with grief.

One cold winter followed another when Katy could barely get fuel. At her praying place, she thanked God for John's friends at the dock who continued to supply her with coal, food, or whatever might be available.

The year 1806 brought wharves crowded with cotton, wool, rice, flour, salt, sugar, and tea. Merchants counted money in their countinghouses or on the piers, and Negro workers could get the contents of any box that broke or spilled. The following year told another tale: embargo. The once-popular Tontine coffeehouse remained empty. To sell her cakes, Katy returned to the streets, standing all day only to return at night weary and often disappointed.

On a clear April morning in 1809, she awoke to the ringing of church bells and the firing of guns throughout the city. Such commotion had not been heard since George Washington marched up Broad Street at war's end, but everyone soon learned that this celebrated the end of the embargo. *Hallelujah!* She thanked God for providing throughout.

Katy opened her door and stepped out into Warren Street, ready to do her shopping. Going east, facing the almshouse, her path took her to Broadway where she turned southward toward the Oswego Market.

To do her marketing, she passed the almshouse. She uttered a prayer for the miserable souls inside who could not pay their debts, some of whose children she saved from the streets. She then pushed her thoughts, like her mother would have done, to the business ahead—baking a graduation cake for Pastor Mitchell's students from Dickinson College to be presented in the morning. She rounded each stall in the market, greeting her favorite merchants and carefully selecting her items.

"Good morning." Katy looked up from the cheese into the proper face of Miss Eliza.

"Good morning, Miss Eliza," she smiled cautiously, remembering how Eliza had helped her after her mother had been sold, and later accused Katy of causing her to lose her job. Still, Eliza was her elder, evidenced by the white hair that rimmed her bonnet and by a chin that had begun to sag. "How are things at the church?"

Eliza had eventually gotten a room at Mrs. Peterson's boardinghouse, where she met another roomer whom she married and with whom she had joined the new Abyssinian Baptist Church.

"Fine. But first, I must apologize for the way I treated you. I was so upset with losin' my job, but 'twasn't really your fault."

"I understand," replied Katy with a lifted brow, "and I accept your apology."

"Thank you; I knew you would." She twisted her hands. "But have you heard the latest news?" Eliza's nervous movements matched her frilly voice.

"Tell me."

"You know, don't you, that your pastor almost got run out of town when he allowed you into the Presbyterian fellowship a few years back. And now him and Missus Graham wanna move your Sunday school into the new church on Murray Street. But the board says they won't give that church another cent if Pastor Mitchell brings those Negroes and ragamuffins in their new building. Missus Graham say if they don't bring 'em in the church, she's gonna bring 'em in her house. Her neighbors said, 'Over our dead bodies.'"

"Bless God!"

"Now, you know the board don't want a fine, up-standin' white woman like Missus Graham havin' 'em in her house, not to mention her neighborhood! That could ruin the city!"

"Well, that explains it. She invited the children there last Sunday. Mrs. Graham herself listened as they recited their catechism then taught them. A glorious time!"

"So it's true!" gulped Eliza. "Missus Graham live with her daughter now, don't she? Did Missus Bethune go along with it?"

"I suppose so," answered Katy.

"How many children did you take to Missus Graham's—I mean, Missus Bethune's house?" asked Eliza, amazed.

"My class is usually about twenty children or how-ever many I can gather from off the streets. Last Sunday I had thirteen."

"How in heaven's name can you care for thirteen children?" gasped Eliza.

"They don't all *live* with me, you know. Three are in the house now. I just placed a boy as an apprentice with the new wheelwright and another as a seamstress with the Bowen family. Both had been with me almost five years!" Lowering her head, she whispered, "Sometimes it's so hard to let them go. Do you remember my Jed? He came to John and me when he was five years old. He's now fourteen and he still comes by to help."

"How many colored you got?" she inquired.

"Usually about half. I started a new meeting on Friday. You should come by, Miss Eliza, and fellowship with us."

"Friday? When you start a meeting on Friday?"

"Very recently. Some of the parents whose children I have helped came to find their children. They decided to stay and learn the Scriptures for themselves, so I invited them to come on Friday. We had three people for the first meeting. Why don't you come by sometime?"

"I ce'tainly will. What time?"

"Seven in the evening."

"Good. By the way, do you remember that Fulani girl who used to roam the streets lookin' for her sister?"

"Of course. Miss Wetchee and I used to see her."

"Well, she's all dressed up now and in her right mind. Goes to Abyssinian Baptist where I go. She even got a name now. It's Nayo."

"Praise God!" Katy exclaimed. "I have prayed many a year for her. I am so *glad* to hear that! Nayo," she repeated.

"Nayo," echoed Miss Eliza. "Good-bye for now. Say hello to Sim for me. And when you see Hendricks, tell him Mr. Schermerhorn is buildin' down on Fulton Street. My husband got work there and they still hirin'."

"Thank you, Eliza. I'll be sure to pass that along. Please, please tell Nayo hello for me." She walked away triumphantly, cheeks aglow, praising God for answered prayer. "Thank You, Jesus, for setting Nayo free!"

A week later, on Friday, Katy awoke at daybreak with a terrible headache. Two hours passed and Hendricks had not come. Somehow she managed to bring in water for the children to wash their faces and sufficient wood to start a fire. But the cupboard held no flour for biscuits, the children's clothes had not been laid out, and neither person she'd asked had come to help this morning. *There it is again,* she thought as she heard a thump outside her front door. She sat up and plopped her feet on the floor. *Lord, please help Callie get well. She's a good girl; You know how much I need her.* She splashed a little water on her face, pulled on her nightcap, and creaked downstairs.

"Anybody there?" she called through the door. In response she heard a shifting movement. Occasionally a drunken man or vagrant would land on her doorstep but rarely so early in the day. So she cautiously released the latch, blinking at the shaft of daylight that shone in.

"Mercy!" Katy exclaimed when she saw two groggy children wearing filthy clothing. "Susie! Get down here! Fast!" She opened the door and pulled them in.

"Ma'am?" questioned a sleepy Susie, peeking her head from the stairway.

"Come help with these children!" A mere eight years old, Susie, who had proven from the beginning to be a willing helper, hopped to her side.

"Take off their clothing! Look them over to see if they have any sores. If not, wash them up and get clean clothes on them. Water is on the bureau. I'll start the porridge." After Katy called Jed to build a fire, she scooped the last of the oats from the bottom of the sack and poured them into a pot of boiling water. As the other children awoke, Susie and Jed helped them wash and dress before they came downstairs. They took their places at the table. Susie brought the two new children last, two boys, around age five. They rushed through their small—but filling—meal of porridge and milk. Morning devotions followed.

The teacher had cleared the long table and pulled the two benches away from it, which she placed at angles near the hearth. She stood before the children to calm them before prayer. A knock came at the door. With great irritation—as her head still throbbed—she asked herself, *What now?* She charged to the door and snatched it open.

"Pastor Mitchell!" she gasped.

"Good morning, Mrs. Ferguson. May I come in?"

"Pastor Mitchell! Why certainly." She stepped aside in a flurry. "Come right in." She wiped her hand on her apron before offering it to the pastor. He grasped and shook it.

"This is Elder Louden, as you know," he said as he stepped inside.

"Good morning, sir." She snapped around and clapped her hands. "Children! Come say 'good morning' to Pastor Mitchell and Elder Louden from the church. Come quickly!" The children scrambled down from the benches and lined up like little soldiers.

Katy went down the line. "This is Jed. This is Tyro. And this is Susie, my helper. She's eight years old but works like a little lady. These two are here for the first time today, Mingo and John." Each child shook both men's hands when introduced.

"You may return to your seats," she ordered. "I'll be

right with you." Then she turned to her guests: "I'd like to offer you a seat. . . ."

"Mrs. Ferguson, we won't be long. I have inquired among the pastors I know throughout the presbytery as well as the city at large. No one has ever heard of a school like yours, a school that invites poor children in on Sunday and teaches them the Scriptures. Yours is the only school of its type in New York, possibly the entire Christian world." He paused.

"Well, sir, I only did what I was led to do. But I appreciate your kind words. . . ."

"The elders at Second Presbyterian have agreed that we would like to join you in this. You should not do this by yourself. Would you like to hold your Sunday school meetings in our new building?"

"Why, sir! I would be so honored! Pastor Mitchell, I never thought . . . I never dreamed . . . I only did . . ."

"Yes, Mrs. Ferguson, you did exactly what is needed to bring about moral change in this city. There's a movement to get more people into church who cannot afford to pay a pew rent. I consider you a pioneer in that movement!"

"I'm so thankful that God would use me."

"You deserve it, Mrs. Ferguson. I've known you since you were a child and can attest to the way God has worked in your life. In fact, when I told the ladies at the church that I was going to pay you a visit, they sent some things—flour, cornmeal, sugar, etc." Her mouth fell open as a carter lugged in three burlap sacks and a five-pound package of butter. "Well, we'll be saying 'good day.' I know you have a lot to think about. But the space will be ready for you in two weeks." Then he leaned around Katy, who stood speechless, and waved good-bye to the children.

"Good-bye, Pastor!"

"Good-bye."

"Pastor, thank you so much. Good day, sirs." Overwhelmed with joy, she sank to her knees in thanksgiving to God for providing space for her school in the new church and for sending the much-needed food. Never had she felt such fulfillment.

Indeed, several years passed before New Yorkers learned of a school similar to Mrs. Ferguson's where poor children were taught Scriptures. It had begun in a poor section of Gloucester, England, among coal miners.

Before her death after a long illness, Mrs. Graham saw Katy's Sunday school firmly established in the new Presbyterian church on Murray Street.

"What you've done will impact the moral education of children for generations to come," she'd proudly told Katy.

Regrettably, Mrs. Graham did not live to attend the wedding of Miss Euphemia Mason, Pastor Mason's eldest daughter, to John Knox. Katy's cake stood at the reception like a white magical castle waiting to be entered. Even the guests remarked at how much Mrs. Graham would have enjoyed seeing it. That wedding cake became the standard by which all wedding cakes after June 1818 were measured.

"Is it as good as the one Katy Ferguson made for Euphemia Mason?" people asked.

Until the day Katy stopped baking, every bride who ordered a cake requested that it be "like the one you baked when Euphemia Mason married John Knox." Katy would smile.

That year stood out in another way. After its meeting, the General Assembly of the Presbyterian Church adopted a strong antislavery resolution, and Robert Bruce officially recorded Katherine Ferguson's manumission from slavery.

Chapter 18

A Decade of Destruction

1830s

A knock came at the door and Sim called out in a weak voice, "I'll get it!" Each of the children had been placed with an apprentice before Christmas, and Katy, upstairs, tidied the vacant rooms. Sim put aside her mending, pulled herself up from her rocking chair near the hearth, hobbled to the door, and opened it wide enough to peek.

"Happy New Year!" sang Luann, her daughter Callie, and George, John's Methodist friend from the dock who recently had been widowed. Behind them came Hendricks with his Coromanti wife, Inger—a woman who gloried in her appearance—wearing a splendid coif.

"Come in! Come in!" scolded Sim. "Cold out there!" Each visitor filed in, putting a warm pot on the table.

Hendricks closed the door and replaced the shaggy quilt across the bottom to keep out drafts. Then he embraced Sim with a warm hug.

"Not too tight! You might break me!" chided Sim through a toothless smile, while prolonging the embrace.

Katy descended the stairs, calling, "Happy New Year!" and rushed to welcome each friend.

"What a joyous way to start the year! Come, sit down! What is this?" she asked, seeing the pots as she motioned her friends to sit on a bench along the table.

"A feast," chimed Callie. "We celebratin' the New Year, your Sunday school being in the Murray Street church and anything else that need celebratin'. Everybody brought something. You sit down, Miss Katy. Momma and I will set up everything."

"Thank You, Jesus. I'll sit right here," answered Katy jovially, taking her usual chair at the head of the table, near the hearth. The two women lifted lids from the pots to reveal roasted chicken, boiled potatoes, string beans, hearth-baked sweet potatoes, and pies for dessert.

"Greenie got a letter from Africa this week," said Hendricks, throwing his leg across the bench to sit.

"Who's that?" asked Inger, patting her hair.

"The gardener at the Presbyterian church," he answered respectfully, then continued to the group. "You 'member that ship the colonizers christened *Mayflower* and sent to Africa with eighty-six free Negroes?"

"Yeah," they recalled.

"Greenie's son went; now Greenie got a letter from

'im. Says it's rough. Hot. Land's hard to farm.'"

"Lotta Negroes don't believe in going back to Africa," stated George. "Druther take they chances here since they already here anyways."

"I would," piped Sim.

"Bet if one of them slave catchers kidnap you, you'da wish you had gone back to Africa," countered Luann.

"Why didn't you go?" asked Hendricks.

"Didden want to. But if a slave catcher kidnap me, I'd prob'ly wish I had!" They all laughed. Callie put out plates, and guests started passing the food, which Katy asked George to bless before they began eating.

"Us Negroes that been free awhile has figured out how to get along. But some who just got they freedom in 1827 ain't doin' too good."

"I cried like a baby at the 'mancipation Day parade."

"Me too," quipped Katy. "Took eight children, and every time a pretty woman marched by each one wanted to know, 'Is that my momma?' I said, 'Ain't I momma enough for y'all?' They each looked up at me and said, 'Yassum.'"

"You a good mother, Katy," said George.

They all agreed, "Yes, you is."

"Thousands of Negroes poured in the city that day, looking for lost relatives."

"Lot of 'em rowdy too," said Sim.

"Some been beat so bad for so long that they can't think no more," explained Hendricks, shaking his head in sorrow.

"Some spend so much time being ridiculous, cuttin'

the fool, that they can't think no mo', neither," Luann said.

"What about you, Miss Katy?" asked Inger. "Do you think Negroes should go back to Africa?"

"The Lord has blessed me right here," answered Katy, piercing a helping of green beans with her fork. A crinkle formed around her lively brown eyes. "But I 'spect He could bless me there as well. Between caring for children, working, and praying for what I need, I don't have time to think much about Africa. Do y'all know what I'd like right now more than anything? A chance to hear Pastor Finney."

"Is that the new white evangelist been preaching all over town?"

"Amen," said Hendricks, standing. "I hear that after the white folks hear him they treat *everybody* better."

"What?"

"His preachin' changes hearts, I tell you. Old man Bolmer left a Finney meeting and gave *three* Negroes jobs."

"Go 'way!"

"*Three* Negroes?"

Three, Hendricks repeated.

"Where he at now?" asked George, rising from his chair, to everyone's amusement. Hendricks sat back down.

"I felt saddened to hear that Pastor Mitchell had passed," lamented Inger. "Has anyone been named to take his place?"

"Pastor Snodgrass is the new pastor. We still miss Pastor Mitchell, but the new reverend is a good man."

The good-natured banter continued until after dusk, when they cleaned up, wished each other a Happy New Year, and went home carrying their empty pots.

New Yorkers continued to be stirred by Pastor Finney while Katy prayed for a chance to hear him. Then one day crossing Fulton Street, she saw Euphemia Knox, Pastor Mason's eldest daughter.

"Katy," she said, "I have good news for you. The evangelist you have been wanting to hear will be coming to a new church near Five Points."

"Pastor Finney? To Five Points! Miss Euphemia, I can hardly believe that a man of the cloth such as Pastor Finney would go anywhere near Five Points."

"It's not like you think, Katy. Remember that old theater on Chatham Street?"

"I do," replied Katy.

"Arthur Tappan put up the money to have it converted to a church and named Charles Finney to pastor it!" Euphemia smiled.

"Bless God! That'll bring the Word right down to the people. But Five Points? Miss Euphemia, it's not safe there—with the gambling and rabble-rousing—but I know Pastor Finney will bring souls to the Lord. That'll make it safer. What will be the name of this church?"

"The Chatham Street Chapel. It's part of the free-church movement, to bring in folks who cannot afford to pay pew rents."

"I'll be praying for the Chatham Street Chapel. And how are the children?"

"Helen has a cold, but otherwise they are fine. How are your children?"

"Jed is preaching now. He first came to us when he was five years old. He still comes back to help me out. He's thirty-eight now and getting gray hair, and he's still skinny . . . unlike me! But he always thought of my late husband as his father. So he's my son."

"You're just big boned, Katy. And it's good to have seen you. I must run, but you have a good day."

"So good to have seen you too, Miss Euphemia."

What Katy did not know was that Jed, now known as Rev. Jethro Snowden, was preaching about her and John. Jed told of them throughout his circuit. He did not know whether he had been lost or abandoned. All he knew is that one day he was alone. He walked out of the door and saw a mob of kids whom he followed. They ended up at a stone house where a woman gave him warm biscuits with syrup, a ripe peach from the windowsill, and cool water. And a man taught him how to make a fire. He always left out the part where he almost knocked over a whole kettle of porridge. But he never forgot that stone house or the couple who lived in it and vowed to repay them if it took the rest of his life.

As though to refute Pastor Finney's godly words, there came to New York a demon in the form of a dread disease. Cholera. Katy and the children lived in the shadow of death, with only the rod of divine Providence and a few sympathizers to help them. Thousands fled the city, merchants shut their doors, and a stranger brought three frightened children to Katy who'd been orphaned by the disease, not even knowing whether they'd caught it. Because Hendricks thought to ask for milk that could not be delivered, because Callie collected the apples a merchant tossed out, and because each brought his commodities to Katy, she had something to set on her table.

On a cool May day when whipped-cream clouds filled a pale blue sky, Charles Finney preached his first sermon at the Chatham Street Chapel. Katy, Callie, and the children sat right there, soaking it all in, being refreshed.

"Hallelujah!" Katy exclaimed, shedding her Presbyterian mold.

"Amen!" Callie's emotions soared with those of the overflowing crowds.

By the sultry night in August when Finney preached his last of seventy sermons, many hearts had been won for Christ. The abolitionists, who wanted slaves freed, rode a wave of triumph. However, less confident colonizationists, who wanted blacks returned to Africa, still fought for it. Violence against Negroes decreased, opening the way for many to improve their lives. Pastor Finney had revived the benevolent heart of the city, but there were those who wanted it oppressive again. Instead of individual successes by blacks serving to destroy negative stereotypes, it had the opposite effect of increasing white antagonism.

These forces soon gathered their strength as angry voices raged in closed rooms throughout the city: *Negroes must be kept in their places! Enough talk about abolition!* On October 1, a yelling, cursing mob of fifteen hundred formed outside of Clinton Hall where a meeting of the Antislavery Society had been called. Fortunately, the Antislavery Society had learned of the proposed mob and moved the meeting uptown to the Chatham Street Chapel, where it was successfully held. But that was only the beginning. By the following summer, pro slavery advocates had amassed in full force.

Something about this don't set right, thought Katy on Monday, July 7, 1834, as she brought the cedar tub to the kitchen, placed it by the hearth, and into it poured water for her bath. She bathed, finished dressing, and put black boots with stout buttons onto her feet, and pulling the two sides together, she fastened them with strong laces drawn crosswise. That past Friday, trouble-makers had planted themselves in the audience at the Antislavery Society's public meeting on July 4. Before Arthur Tappan could finish reading the declaration of sentiments, demonstrators began hooting so the audience could not hear the speaker. They hissed, stamped their feet, and became so boisterous that he could not continue. People left the meeting in disgust while demonstrators cheered. *And now here I am getting dressed to go to another anniversary celebration for our emancipation.*

"Let's go on," she said to Jed when he arrived to get her, expressing concerns about her going. Noise filled the drab, barnlike chapel. Katy, nearing sixty, climbed to the galleries in the mixed audience to take a seat, with Jed beside her. Before the program even began, several angry white men rushed to the stage. Before a startled audience, they ambushed the Negro dignitaries and tried to oust them through a side door. However, the dignitaries-turned-defenders overpowered the mob, herded them through the chapel, and pushed them out the door, to the hushed delight of the audience. When everyone settled down, the program resumed with a choir singing a new hymn by John Greenleaf Whittier. Within moments, someone began randomly throwing prayer books, one of which struck Katy on the head.

"Ooow," she cried, falling forward. Jed jumped up and was grazed by a hymnal. He flung his arms around Katy.

"Let's get outta here!" he shouted, leading her out while flying books skimmed over the audience, and angry whites called out, "Negroes, go home!" Fortunately, watchmen arrived from the mayor's office in time to prevent further disorder, and the crowd returned home safely. After Jed left and returned to the church where he'd been working, Katy sat at the table holding ice to her head when Hendricks arrived to deliver a pail of milk.

"Did you hear what else happened last night?" he asked, after asking about Katy's injury.

"What?"

"Rioters broke into Lewis Tappan's house."

"Was anyone hurt?"

"The Tappans were not at home. So the mob broke the windows and mirrors, threw their furniture into the street, and set fire to it."

"My Lord," sighed Katy.

"But someone sounded an alarm; the firemen came and put out the blaze."

"Let's all gather at the meeting on Friday, and we'll give this over to the Lord."

Luann, Callie, Hendricks, and a few others gathered

around Katy's table to begin praying for an end to the tension that crackled and sparked throughout the city. As they bowed their heads, a furious knock pounded on the door, and Lucy Pugh got up to open it. Tyro leaned against the doorpost, panting.

"They attacked Pastor Cox's church! Broke out the winders!"

"Who?" the group chorused.

"Mobs! They all over the place!" said Tyro, catching his breath.

"On Laight Street! Why Pastor Cox?" asked Lucy. All eyes turned to Katy.

"Do you remember what happened several months ago? Arthur Tappan and Samuel Cornish met on Laight Street and went into Pastor Cox's church to sit and talk. Remember?"

"I do," replied Luann, "because certain chu'ch peoples threatened to resign their membership 'cause Mr. Tappan brought a Negro in their white church."

"Sam Cornish whiter den some o' dem!" said Callie.

Tyro picked up where he left off: "They lef' there and hit the Presbyter'an church on Spring Street!"

"Pastor Ludlow's church?"

"Yeah! Then they tore down Peter Williams's chu'ch and his house 'cause they say he pe'formed a marriage 'twixt black and white. They got him far it. They chained a row of carts, wagons, barrels, and ladders across the street to stop the 'thorities from gettin' to 'em. Then they commenced to throwin' rocks at the chu'ch. They smashed the doors and winders and made a rush inside and tore up the organ, the pulpit, and turned over the pews."

"My God!" the shocked group responded.

"When the police broke 'em up, they ran up Laurens Street to the pastor's house and broke out the winders and doors on his house."

"Mercy!"

"Didden I say I heard the sound of breaking glass?" Callie said to Katy.

"You sho'ly did. I heard strange noises too," Hendricks chimed in. Another knock came at the door, and Luann's cousin who lived in the Quarter had more news.

"A mob ran through the Quarter and broke out the windows at Zion church! Glass all over the place. Then they got the Baptist church—"

"Abyssinian? Where 'liza goes?" Hendricks interrupted.

"Yeah, 'liza and Nayo. Then they broke down the doors and windows at Pastor Williams's house—"

"How big was the mob?" asked Hendricks.

"Hundreds of 'em. Then I seen 'em running up Mulberry Street, knocking over flower boxes, kicking over steps—"

"Where was you?" they said in unison on the edge of their seats.

"Hidin' in the alley 'til they lef'. Then I ran down here 'cause I knew they wouldn't come down this far. Up on Elm Street, they pulling down people's roofs and hauling they furniture out in the street!"

"What about the Mut'al Relief Society on Orange Street?" asked Katy.

"They got that too."

"What about the barbershop?" Hendricks wondered out loud.

"Davis tried to scare them off by waving his musket! But they . . . shot him."

Everyone became silent and morose, stricken by the thoroughness of the violence, the sacredness of its targets, and the innocence of its victims. Poor Davis. Tears rolled down many cheeks.

"Let us look to the Lord," offered Katy. Everyone quieted themselves and bowed for prayer. They went around and around, each person naming a friend or relative or a household, and asked for God's protection.

"Jus' hep us, Lord!" said Lucy.

"Lord, have mercy!" muttered others.

When they'd said all they wanted to say, Katy ended with, "We ask these things in the name of our Savior, Jesus Christ. Amen." When they peeked out the window, all seemed quiet, so they went home.

The next day throughout the Quarter, Five Points, and at every home where an abolitionist or Negro sympathizer lived, the sound of brooms sweeping glass rasped through the air. Here and there wafted smoke from burning furniture. At the Presbyterian churches on Spring and Varick Streets, white men swept up the fragments of organs, pews, hymnals, candles, and sacred cloths that lay soiled and desecrated in the streets.

Except for an occasional brawl during the 1835 elections, peace returned the following year. Then on a September day when Tyro visited, Katy asked him to take a pan of gingerbread to David Ruggles's bookstore on Lipensard Street. Tyro ran all the way back with news that arsonists had burned down the store, having learned that it harbored fugitive slaves. As destruction begat destruction, more news was yet to come.

On a bitter, cold night in December as tempestuous winds banked snow along the streets, lurid lights streamed into the sky dropping sparks below on Wall Street. Residents awakened by the ringing of alarms saw firemen hastening to the fire. River water froze in the hoses before it reached the blaze and buildings tumbled like avalanches. Hundreds of bystanders huddled, wrapped in blankets like cocoons, and watched helplessly for hours until, at 2:00 A.M., Mayor Lawrence decided to halt the inferno by blowing up the buildings that remained in its path. Only then was the fire stopped.

The next day dawned upon a stunned and weeping city. Katy and the children walked among the disillusioned crowds to see the seventeen blocks laid waste by the fire. These included homes as well as stores that had previously sold hardware, crockery, dry goods, European imports, umbrellas, clothing, drugs, groceries, shoes, glass, books, tin, and tobacco.

Katy strained to locate what had been Arthur Tappan's dry goods store and the businesses of several regular customers. Whole blocks lay in smoldering ruin. Though her house had been spared, the homes of many of her customers hadn't. In this atmosphere of danger and destruction, she pondered the future of this city she had come to love, the people and businesses that had been displaced, and what might lie ahead.

"Miss Katy, can we pick through da rubble to see if

we can fin' anything?"

"No!" screamed Katy, her voice cracking in a way that caused the children to look up at her. They saw a hardness in her face they'd never seen before. She remembered the last day she had seen her mother, leaving home to glean in the rubble of a fire. *Put that behind you*. She stooped to gather the children in her arms.

"Why can't we, Miss Katy?" a boy asked, wiggling against her tight embrace.

Holding him firmly, she responded, "Slave catchers might get you. Let's go home."

Chapter 19

The Mysterious Long, Black Schooner

1839–1841

*K*aty listened from the second seat in the left pew, the one usually reserved for her and her diverse brood. Pastor Snodgrass ended his sermon by asking for prayer on behalf of forty-four African slaves who had revolted aboard a Spanish ship called the *Amistad*. Her eyebrows rose to attention. The schooner now floated off the coast of Connecticut, and the Africans simmered in a New Haven jail, awaiting the court's decision as to their fate: return them to the men from whom they had escaped or set them free.

Her heart leaped and her hand quickened her fan against the humid air. When church ended, she anxiously scanned the departing congregation for Arthur Tappan, whom she soon located near the door, surrounded by several men standing in rapt attention. Katy shushed the children, sat quietly, and listened.

This is what she heard: A mysterious long, black schooner had been spotted offshore in Long Island Sound. The captain of a survey brig had sailed to it and found it manned by Negroes. Holding the Negroes at gunpoint, the survey crew boarded the ship, searched it, and discovered two Spaniards.

The Spaniards reported that they had purchased the captives in Cuba and were taking them to plantations near Puerto Principe. However, the Negroes, led by a man named Cinque, had gotten free and armed themselves, killed the Spanish crew, and taken over the ship. These two Spaniards had been spared to steer the ship to Africa. By day, they did as they were told and steered east toward Africa, but at night they altered the course, sailing north. After two months of zigzagging in the Atlantic, with supplies almost depleted, the *Amistad* reached Long Island Sound.

"The latest news," said Tappan, "is that crew members from the survey brig towed the *Amistad* to Connecticut." Most men listened in silence, occasionally rubbing their chins or squinting their eyes with concern.

"We'll see what happens next," concluded a whiskered gentleman, pulling a watch from his fob pocket to check the time. They began to disperse.

"Mr. Tappan," called Katy graciously after she had sent the children outside. "May I have a word with you?"

"Katy, how good to see you." He turned to face her.

"The news of the Africans is quite interesting. . . ."

"It's quite a story, Katy, and I assure you, I'm going to do all I can to see that they are sent back home. I know that you are a praying woman, and I ask that you pray for these men," he said, "and girls."

"Girls?" asked Katy, her face flushed with surprise.

"Yes, there were three girls on the schooner ranging in age from eleven to thirteen. They were well cared for. The Africans' leader had become like a father to them."

Katy could not conceal a smile. Left alone in the hands of white traders, she imagined, the girls may have been . . . God knows what may have happened to them.

He gave her a few other details. "I will be calling on you in the coming days," he concluded.

"I'll help in any way I can."

The next day, Katy headed north toward the Quarter to call on Mrs. Peterson. Reaching the tiny porch, she knocked and opened the door. Several boarders sat around the large oak table, where they wiped their sweat and talked about the *Amistad*. Mr. Low, the least-popular boarder, spoke.

"Shame de way dose African savages kilt all dem white sailors."

Low's remarks struck a weary chord in the heart of Gerret, who devoted his life to helping escaped slaves get to Canada. Gerret had long since given up on trying to talk sense into Low regarding the Negroes' plight.

"Do you think de Africans should'a kept still and let themselves be sold into slavery, Low?"

"Low prob'ly thinks dey should'a squeezed a bit tighter in the bottom o' dat stinkin' ship so's de sailors could'a wedged in a few mo'."

"Yeah, den de leader, Cinque, could'a brung along his chirren so dey could be slaves too."

"Y'all don't understand," countered Low, defending himself. "Dem Africans *belonged* to dem sailors. It's one thang iffen dey had owned demselves. But dey was *prope'ty*. Here come Miss Katy. She can 'splain it."

"Good afternoon, Miss Katy," said each of the four men and two women. The men pushed back their chairs and rose to greet her. A woman said, "Low's body been freed but his fool mind still in slavery."

"I understand that Tappan has gotten lawyers for the Africans," said Gerret, directing his remarks to Katy.

"Yes, now we have to pray for the outcome of the case. I hope to see you all on Friday at the prayer meeting," spoke Katy cheerily. Without response, they sat and renewed their conversation. Mrs. Ferguson and Mrs. Peterson moved to the front porch where they sipped lemonade and shared thoughts on the *Amistad*.

"Who's helping Tappan?" asked Mrs. Peterson.

"Pastor Jocelyn and Pastor Levitt, along with Tappan's younger brother, Lewis."

"Who they got as lawyers?"

"A man from Connecticut plus lawyers Staples and Sedgewick from here."

"Don't Nettie cook for a lawyer named Staples?" she asked. "Reckon it's the same family?"

"We'll soon find out," replied Katy, "but they can't do anything without the Lord. I'll be praying for them night and day, and taking up an offering too. Tappan says there are three little girls among them."

"Go 'way," responded Mrs. Peterson.

Katy continued, "But no women."

"Count me in," replied Mrs. Peterson, sipping her lemonade. "I'll pray!"

Katy rejoiced, said, "Thank you," and affirmed their friendship with a touch of Mrs. Peterson's hand.

"I'm sorry that these boarders don't come to your meetin'," she whispered, leaning toward Katy.

"They been free so long," Katy replied. "Most who come to pray still remember the chains that kept them slaves. They still have nightmares about their shackles, or else they come giving thanks that they escaped, or because they want to pray for family members still in slavery. Seems like once the danger passes, they get a little comfortable and don't come to pray anymore. I thank God for those who do."

At the Friday prayer meeting, Katy asked each person, including the children, to pray for two or three of the captives, having Callie briefly mention each one from the list Tappan had given her.

"We'll pray for the father and son named Pie and Fuli," offered Henry. His wife, Betty, nodded in agreement when he added, "Plus the other three boys." Katy prayed for the Africans' leader, Cinque, the committee, and eight of the men. She asked the children to pray for the three little girls: Teme, Dagne, and Margru, remembering the precious daughters, Abigail and Julia, who were taken from her. And so they chose names until all forty-four captives had been accounted for.

Feeling poorly for several days, Sim had crept upstairs and gone to bed early, before the prayer meeting started. Katy had been worried about her for days and spoon-fed her chicken broth. "I's tired," she'd whispered that morning but had insisted on coming partways downstairs to greet the praying folks. "Pray for me, Katherine," she called before she struggled back upstairs. The following morning Susie discovered her body.

For months afterward, Katy's shoulders sagged with grief. Twice she'd lost Miss Sim, and this time was final. Callie eventually moved in with her and arranged for her Friday evening meetings to continue and for her Sunday school classes to convene. Katy didn't take in any new children, and those with her spent days in front of the house playing hopscotch, leapfrog, and blindman's bluff.

All Katy did was bake, and her baking did not suffer. She whipped out her anguish in fresh eggs that firmed into the smooth custards with which she filled buns. She churned butter with a vigor that yielded fluffy frosting for her cakes. She tossed, pounded, and rolled her dough, raising little puffs of flour that sifted down to be received in her hand again.

At night she listened intently as Callie told her all that had happened that day. Then Callie would read her a chapter from the Bible, as was their custom each evening. Following her prayers, she'd fall off to sleep, a welcome respite from her grief and labors.

The winter of her sixty-seventh year, despite Callie's presence, Katy felt lonely and isolated. Luann had followed Sim in death, while both Hendricks and Mrs. Peterson suffered gout and rarely came out.

In January 1840, as men worked to chip the city free from a coat of ice, God answered a prayer. Katy lingered after church one Sunday and Mr. Tappan approached her.

"I have news for you, Mrs. Ferguson. The *Amistad* Africans won their case in the circuit court in Connecticut. . . ." his brisk voice trailed off.

"Thank You, Jesus," she exclaimed, clasping her hands together.

"But the prosecutors are going to appeal that decision," he added matter-of-factly. The Africans, it had turned out, were Mende, Katy's countrymen. Among them could very well have been the sons of her people.

"What can I do to help?" she responded, beginning to feel invigorated by this cause.

"Mrs. Ferguson, we need a miracle. This case is going all the way to the Supreme Court of the United States. President Van Buren knew exactly what he was doing when he had this case sent up. Of the nine justices, five are from the South, strong supporters of slavery. I know you are a praying woman, and if anyone can win God's favor, it's you. I'm planning to send Pastor Bacon to prayer meetings around the city to explain our problem and get folks praying for a miracle. When can he come to yours?"

"This Friday," she stated without hesitation or doubt. "Those Mendes been winning so far, ain't they?"

"Yes," replied Tappan.

"They gonna keep on winning!"

"Mrs. Ferguson, I admire your faith!"

"And I yours, Mr. Tappan."

When Pastor Bacon, a short, chubby white man, entered Katy Ferguson's house on Warren Street, a hush fell upon the assembled Negroes. Pastor Bacon put them at ease with his friendliness and thanked them for coming. He asked that they pray for the justices by name, which Callie had written down. Pastor Bacon repeated their names aloud: "Taney, Story, Thompson, McLean, Baldwin—"

"Pardon me. I thought Baldwin was the lawyer!" interrupted Henry, the most outspoken prayer warrior.

"The lawyer is *Roger* Baldwin; this is a different Baldwin. He needs extra prayer because they say his mind wanders." Pastor Bacon winked at the group.

"You mean he tetched?" asked Henry. The women tittered. Not knowing the meaning of "tetched," Pastor Bacon turned to Katy.

She smiled and nodded, "Yes, Baldwin is tetched. His mind wanders."

Pastor Bacon continued. "The other judges are Wayne, Barbour, Catron, and McKinley. The lawyer working with Roger Baldwin is a former president, John Quincy Adams." An approving murmur emanated from the prayer group, impressed that a former president should be called in. "He came out of retirement to take this case," continued Pastor Bacon with pride. "Please pray that the men will be merciful and wise in their decision."

Concluding his remarks, the reverend asked, "Would you like to add anything, Mrs. Ferguson?"

"Yes," she replied, coming forward. "The Mendes aboard that ship want desperately to go back to their own country, same as our ancestors did when first captured and brought to 'merica. We have a chance to help them by asking God to be with them and stand by them. Most of us were born here and this is all we know. But those men and children have families back home, a land, a language, a way of life, a country they love. They have already showed their strength and bravery.

"Though we be free, we are one breath away from being caught by a drunken blackbirder, snuck out of New York, and sold South. For many of you, the blood of the lash still glistens on your backs. But let us remember the 'postle Paul who, while in jail, prayed not because of the dark or cold or because he was hongry. He prayed for others that they might be strengthened. Now let us do the same for our brethren who are jailed in New Haven, so that they may be freed by the courts and can go home. Amen."

They bowed their heads and said, "Amen."

The prayer group, Henry and Betty, Anna, Lucy, Callie, and a few others, sat around Katy's table three weeks later to recount events of the prior weeks. Hendricks, who was feeling good, was also there. On the table, which was surrounded by smiling faces, sat small tin plates of gingerbread slathered with whipped cream. Some knew the story but loved telling it and hearing it. Hendricks began.

"On February 22, 1841, the trial began with the court made up of nine judges, five who could not wait to get the Mende Africans out of jail and back in slavery and four likely to vote for their freedom. The co'troom was packed. Peoples jammed in every whichaway. But when they looked up at the bench, the judge from Alabama wasn't there. The Lord heard y'all's prayers and kept that white man in Alabama. That made the count four to four."

"Amen!"

"Hallelujah!" Betty, Anna, and Lucy reached for a square of gingerbread, and Callie kept the tea flowing.

"Next day the lawyers argued back and forth, back and forth. The count still stood at four to four."

"That's when Miss Katy got down on her knees!" quipped Henry.

"Satan, look out!" added Betty.

"I knew somethin' was gonna happen then."

"Soon as Miss Katy's knees hit the flo', the Lord asked, 'What you want, Miss Katy?'" Katy chuckled at their teasing.

"Miss Katy said, 'Lord, we want the right thing to happen. The thing that will please You.' Next thing you know, one of them judges just up and died!"

"Hush yo' lying, Hendricks!" countered Lucy.

"Ain't no lie. Right, Miss Katy?"

"One of the judges died! You didden know?"

"No! He died?" asked Lucy.

"Died. The Lord said, 'Brother, yo' time is up . . . now.'"

"Thank You, Jesus!" they shouted. Anna wept.

"Then the count was four to three," continued Hendricks, "in favor of the Mende Africans."

"Is that when the court took a recess?" asked Henry.

"To honor the dead."

"That was the longest week in my life."

188

"Meanwhile, y'all kept on praying. Then the seven came back." Hendricks paused for dramatic effect.

"What happened next?" asked Betty, edging forward on her chair.

"Justice Story marched in, wearing his long black robe and white wig. He told the thirty-eight Mende Africans, 'Stand up!' Six had died. So still you could hear a cart wheel squeak on the other side of town. Justice Story announced the decision. The Mende Africans! Free! Six judges voted to free them and one against."

"God answers prayer! Hallelujah! What a victory!"

"Which one didden vote to free 'em?" Hendricks looked to Katy for the answer.

"The one that was tetched," she smiled. The prayer warriors whooped.

"What a blessed day in the Lord! Thank You."

"Thank You, Jesus!"

"I seen the Lord's hand. I'm ready to die now," whimpered Anna.

"I ain't," said Lucy. "Every time I see God do one good thing, I want to see two or three more!"

"Amen!" They rejoiced, pleased that justice had swayed her scales in their favor.

Anna turned to Katy and asked, "What's gonna happen to the Mendes now?"

"The committee gonna find a way to get 'em back to Africa. So we ain't through praying yet. But they want them to go as missionaries. Pastor Ludlow and three students at Yale College teach them from the Bible."

Katy never saw Hendricks alive after that meeting. Arthritis nearly confined him to his house, and pneumonia took his life. Meanwhile, word came that Tyro had been jailed.

The slave trade between Africa and America yielded obscene profits to many European and American merchants. However, after federal law ended the practice, an illicit trade continued, with much of its cargo destined for New York City. Men who smuggled in slaves were called blackbirders and one of their favorite rendezvous was Sweet's Restaurant at Fulton and South Streets. As Tyro walked in this vicinity talking to no one but himself, a disturbance broke out. An angry constable seized him and jailed him with the lot. Katy depleted her meager savings to have Tyro released, securing the lifelong devotion of his family. But he never recovered from the trauma of it, and it eventually cost him his life.

After the court awarded their freedom, the Mendes were housed in Connecticut at a key station on the Underground Railroad. During the summer, they sold tablecloths and napkins they had made to raise money for the passage home. That fall Pastor Wilson came to speak at Katy's prayer meeting on the Mendes' behalf.

"Our prayer," he uttered, "is to send these Africans back as missionaries, to tell the African people about Jesus Christ. Every missionary society now in existence in America sanctions slavery. Slaveholding men preach from their pulpits. This is an outrage against Jesus' teachings. We are taking this opportunity to form a mission agency made up primarily of Africans to open a mission in Africa. We call it the Union Missionary Society.

Five Mendes are charter members. Our dear Brother Pennington is the founder.

"We are in a race against time to raise money to send the Mendes back home before good sailing weather ends. President Tyler has refused to allow them passage on an American warship. Neither would Great Britain return them home, though the government promised assistance upon the group's arrival at Sierra Leone. Two missionaries agreed to accompany them. Tappan has taken the group on tours throughout New England to raise money for the trip. Now they are coming to the Broadway Tabernacle in New York. Thank you for your prayers and I invite you all to the Broadway Tabernacle."

On the stage sat two pastors of local churches along with the committee who had worked with the Mendes for two years, and several divinity students from Yale College. Before a crowd of nearly five thousand people, the Mende men sang an antislavery hymn, followed by the children who showed their skills at arithmetic and spelling. Katy's children wept when Margru, one of the little girls for whom they had prayed, recited Psalm 100. A speech in Mende by Cinque, which recounted the heroic mutiny with vivid gestures and tones, crowned the evening.

"Send them back—not as slaves but as missionaries!" challenged Tappan. Katy felt the presence of the Holy Spirit in the room and was so lifted that when she stood, her feet barely touched the ground.

The Mendes sailed from New York Harbor in November aboard the *Gentleman*.

Chapter 20

A Be-Still Bakery

1842–1852

"*H*ere I am seventy years old and finally the Lord gives me my own bakery!" The store faced Thompson Street. In the large middle room behind the store stood a stone hearth with an oven on the outside wall and a pantry. In back of the store, a comfortable kitchen.

"I'm so happy for you, Mother Ferguson," gushed Susie, now married with two daughters. She and her grandchildren sat opposite Katy in the kitchen sampling star-shaped sugar cookies.

"'Weeping endures for a night but joy comes in the morning!' My sole regret is that Mrs. Peterson and so many other dear friends did not live to see it!"

"Great-Grandmother Ferguson, may I have another

cookie, pleeeese?" asked Mary.

"Yes, baby, here you are," replied Katy, passing the platter across the table.

"Mother Ferguson, a colored woman named Sojourner Truth is coming to town. Jehu and I are going to hear her."

"As long as she speaks truth," replied Katy. "And I've heard she does."

"The children and I must leave now." Susie moved to gather her things. "I'm sorry I couldn't come to your grand opening yesterday but am glad it was a success."

"I'm overjoyed that you came today," Katy replied as she raised herself from the chair to walk them to the door.

"We'll be back soon. Children, come kiss your Great-Grandmother Ferguson."

"Take these cookies to eat, children. You have a long walk home ahead of you."

"The Quarter ain't far, Great-Grandmother," they protested.

"It's far to me, darling. But it makes me all the more happy when you come to see me. Don't forget to say your prayers at night."

"We won't. Good-bye."

Chapter 21

A Crown Awaits

1853

Katy opened the door to her bakery, releasing the rich fragrance of a pineapple upside down cake, a pound cake, and a tray of cherry-studded crullers. There stood Cato, now old and bent, with a message from Lewis Tappan and a small crate of Bibles.

"Dese some Bibles for slaves, ma'am. After you given 'em out we have others. Cake sure smells good."

"Thank you, Cato. Come to the kitchen and have a slice."

"Now you know I would like dat, Miss Katy. I always make dis my las' stop so I can do jus' dat. And I got news, good news 'bout a colored man comin' to New York. His name is Frederick Douglass, ma'am, and wit' all due respect, 'cause you know I think de world of you, but dis man, Frederick Douglass, he don't have no truck wit' dis business of Bibles for slaves. He say, 'Give slaves freedom. Slaves don't need nothin' but freedom.' And I mus' say, ma'am, I agree wit' dat.'"

"Um," Katy replied as she removed from her oven the buttery crowned pound cake, which she took to the kitchen and placed on the round table that almost filled the room. Cato followed.

"Ma'am, I was downtown yesterday, and dey's bringing in slaves so fas' you wouldn't believe it. It ain't no different now den it was back in 1808. Dey don' even try to hide it. And Frederick Douglass say it got to stop. We want freedom now! For all!"

"Where is Frederick Douglass from, Cato?"

"Don' rightly know. But I know he a man o' God . . . like you a woman o' God, the way you taken care o' poor li'l chirren all dese years. Dat's God's work!"

"The laborers are few."

Silence fell upon the room as the two sat and sipped milk from earthenware cups and savored the golden pound cake.

"I'm slowin' down now, Cato; can't do like I used to. But without Mr. Tappan and the abolitionists, the road would have been rougher, so I guess I can give out a few Bibles for His cause."

"Yes, ma'am."

"Word of God can do only good; it cannot do bad."

"If you can read it."

"I can't read it, Cato, but I can live it. I regret that I cannot read it, and I hold Massa Bruce accountable before God for it too."

"I look to de day when colored can read it *and* live it."

"What a blessed day that will be!"

"Miss Katy, Mr. Tappan wants you to go to Augustus Washington's daguerreotype studio on Fulton Street to sit for a portrait," said Cato, stopping by the bakery on his way to meet Jed.

"Please sit still, Mrs. Ferguson."

"I'm trying very hard, Mr. Washington, but my boy, Jed, is coming home today and I can hardly keep myself still."

"I understand; it won't be much longer." Augustus Washington went behind the box, draped his head and body under a black cloth attached to the camera, and located Mrs. Ferguson's angelic face encircled by a lace cap.

"Jed," Katy uttered with a smile a few moments later, "is gonna read the letter I received from the Mende missions on Friday."

"Jed?" Mr. Washington lifted the cloth and looked around the contraption.

"Yes! My boy, my son. I got word that he's coming home this week and I can't be sitting here while you point that thing at me. I must prepare for my son. He's been preaching up in Albany. He first came to me and my husband when he was five years old. Now he's almost as old as me. You ever heard of him?"

"What's his name again?"

"Jed. Reverend Jethro Snowden."

"I may have heard the name once or twice."

"I've been praying. He's gonna run the bakery God gave me—maybe then he'll put on a pound or two—and help Callie keep the school going. Callie says he'll be a real asset. Neither one of them married."

"Imagine that," said the photographer and lifted the cloth over his head. "You're blessed, Mrs. Ferguson."

"Don't I know it!"

"Be very still, Mrs. Ferguson." Whoosh! The flash exploded.

One day as Katy prepared to wash the children and send them off to school, Cato rapped at the back door.

"Miss Katy, I's here to tell you that Mr. Tappan will call on you at yo' house here on Friday at three o'clock. Is you goin' to be home?"

"Cato, Mr. Tappan knows full well that I have a Bible study here at my house every Friday and been doing it for the last thirty-five years. Are you sure he said Friday?"

"Mr. Tappan, he said Thursday, ma'am, Thursday."

"What's wrong, Cato? Are you all right?"

"Miss Katy, I's heartbroken. Frederick Douglass, he wrote a book, an' I can't read it. I can't read. I've tried to, but I can't."

"Come in, Cato, and sit a spell. I understand how you feel. . . . Isn't your grandson, Sam, learning to read?"

"Yas."

"See?" Katy consoled. "Don't you worry. He will read that book to you. You make sure Sam gets his lessons, and he will read that book to you. Mr. Douglass's words will not be lost."

"Thank you, ma'am. I feel better. If I can't learn to read, my grandchildren will, and they will read to me."

Late in the evening, Callie read the Bible to Katy. Its God-breathed words and Hebraic rhythms soothed her soul like a balm. She reclined in her rocker with her eyes closed and her skirts trailing the floor, taking in the words—words that spread like a balm over the cut made by a sharp rebuke, the stab of an unfair epithet, and the sting of a man's refusal to let her pass on the sidewalk. Callie read and the words rose like an aromatic balm. The words soothed her, relieving the ache in her arms and legs and lifting the weight of the world from her soul.

One evening after Callie finished reading and closed her Bible, she looked up at Katy, who did not move. Katy was motionless in her rocker with her head tilted slightly forward. An alarm rose in Callie's breast. She ran to the front of the house, opened the door, and called for help.

A great cloud of witnesses filled the Scottish Presbyterian Church where Katy had received Communion more than sixty years earlier. The air was fragrant with flowers and the organ hummed in hushed, comforting tones. Muffled sobs and the rustle of slow movement were the only other sounds. Candles placed high up on the walls flickered light over the heads of the mourners.

Everyone was there. Her church members and all the children from her Sunday school came: Susie, Jed, and Cato—to whom Katy had given shelter when they were children—and their families. Members of the Friday prayer meeting group: Henry, Betty, Anna, Lucy, and others. Boarders from Mrs. Peterson's boardinghouse. George's children also came. George had worked with Katy's husband at the docks and was too weak to attend but sent his family. The Fulani girl, Nayo, hobbled in on a cane. "To God be the glow-ry!" she whispered repeatedly.

Afterward, when the mourners sat around Katy's table, they remembered Hendricks and speculated about how proud he would have been for him and his horse, Tulip, to lead Katy's funeral procession. They talked about Sim and how she was known for her beautiful clothing until Katy got a hold of her. Then she was known for her beautiful spirit. They recalled how Tyro talked all the time. It was necessary to request a moment of silence to make him stop. They spoke of Miss Eliza and Callie's mother, Luann. They mentioned Mrs. Isabella Graham and her daughter who helped Katy get her freedom.

Jed added logs to the fireplace while Callie replaced the large, round candle on the table that had melted down onto the plate.

"Katy never forgot that old schooner that her mother escaped on. Sometimes she would just stand and look out over the river. 'Look! There's a schooner,' she would say. 'Maybe it brought runaway slaves from Virginia.'"

"Every year she sold the most goods at Pinkster."

"... and told the most people about Jesus."

"She never forgot her mother's friends, either: Miss Wetchee, Miss Sim, and Mr. Hendricks."

"She never tired of thanking God for them. She always said, 'I could not have survived without them.'"

"What about Pastor Mason?"

"Oh, she loved Pastor Mason," they all agreed.

"Remember how she said her knees trembled when she first went to talk with him about her soul? But, hallelujah, he accepted her. Even gave her Communion with the congregation."

"How about that wedding cake she baked for his daughter?"

"I saw it! It was the most beautiful cake you ever saw! And to taste it was pure heaven."

"Nobody ever forgot that cake! She wouldn't let just any-old-body deliver her cakes, either. Had to be Mr. Wilkes or Hendricks. If anybody else came to pick one up, she'd say, 'Where's Mr. Wilkes?' or 'Where's Mr. Hendricks?' You dare not try to deliver her cakes 'less you was one of them."

"Ah, Miss Katy," someone sighed. "She was so happy doing the Lord's work."

"I never saw her happier than when those *Amistad* Africans sailed back home."

"She prayed all the time . . . never complained . . . 'cept when somebody wasted some food."

"Yeah!" they all laughed. "Clean your plate!"

"Her school was the first Sunday school in the state of New York. And ain't no person told her to open a Sunday school. It came from the Lord!"

Everybody said, "Amen! Yes, Lord!"

"Everything was 'for the children.'"

"She's with the angels now."

The group became quiet. Then several among them began to gather their things to go home.

"Don't worry about the kitchen," Callie assured them. "I'll clean up."

"I'll help," said Susie's granddaughter. She removed an apron from her purse, put it on, and began gathering the empty plates.

"What about her work for the Lord?" someone asked. "Who's going to take it up?"

"Jed and I been talking about that," said Callie.

"We can't let it stop with her death," replied Jed.

"I can sell cakes," offered Lucy's daughter, "to help keep things going."

"I'm learning the Scriptures," said Cato's grandson. "I can help out."

"Me too," offered others. "We can help."

Jed and Callie turned to each other and smiled. Their hearts grieved with the loss of their friend, but their spirits warmed with hope for the future.

MORE THAN A SLAVE TEAM

ACQUIRING EDITOR:
Cynthia Ballenger

COPY EDITOR:
Kathleen M. Humphries

BACK COVER COPY:
Julie Allyson-Ieron, Joy Media

COVER DESIGN:
Lydell A. Jackson

INTERIOR DESIGN:
Ragont Design

PRINTING AND BINDING:
Dickinson Press Incorporated

The typeface for the text of this book is
Sabon